More praise for
EDUARDO HALFON'S FICTION

"Elegant." —*Marie Claire*

"Engrossing." —**NBC Latino**

"Fantastic." —**NPR *Alt.Latino***

"Deeply accessible, deeply moving."
—*Los Angeles Times*

"Offer[s] surprise and revelation at every turn."
—*Reader's Digest*

"One senses Kafka's ghost, along with Bolaño's, lingering in the shadows. . . . [Halfon's] books, which take on such dark subjects, are so enjoyable to read." —*New York Review of Books*

"[Halfon's hero] delights in today's risible globalism, but recognizes that what we adopt from elsewhere makes us who we are."
—*New York Times Book Review*

"With [Halfon's] slender but deceptively weighty books, which are at once breezy and melancholic, bemused and bitter, he opens up worlds to readers in return." —*Kirkus Reviews*

Canción

Canción

Eduardo Halfon

Translated from the Spanish by
Lisa Dillman & Daniel Hahn

BELLEVUE LITERARY PRESS
New York

First published in the United States in 2022
by Bellevue Literary Press, New York

For information, contact:
Bellevue Literary Press
90 Broad Street
Suite 2100
New York, NY 10004
www.blpress.org

"The Conference," "The Bedouin," "Canción," and "Kimono on the Skin" were
originally published in Spanish in 2021 in *Canción* by Libros del Astroide.

Translation © 2022 by Lisa Dillman and Daniel Hahn

The author would like to thank Columbia University's Institute for Ideas and
Imagination and also the Wissenschaftskolleg zu Berlin for their support in the
writing of this book.

An early version of "Canción" was previously published in the *New York Review
of Books*.

This is a work of fiction. Characters, organizations, events, and places (even
those that are actual) are either products of the author's imagination or are used
fictitiously.

Library of Congress Cataloging-in-Publication Data

Names: Halfon, Eduardo, author. | Hahn, Daniel, translator. |
   Dillman, Lisa, translator.
Title: Canción / Eduardo Halfon ; translated from the Spanish by Lisa
   Dillman & Daniel Hahn.
Other titles: Canción. English
Description: First edition. | New York : Bellevue Literary Press, 2022.
Identifiers: LCCN 2022020505 | ISBN 9781954276079 (paperback ; acid-free
   paper) | ISBN 9781954276086 (ebook)
Subjects: LCGFT: Novels.
Classification: LCC PQ7499.3.H35 C36513 2022 | DDC
   863/.7--dc23/eng/20220429
LC record available at https://lccn.loc.gov/2022020505

Bellevue Literary Press would like to thank all its generous donors—individuals
and foundations—for their support.

This publication is made possible by the New York
State Council on the Arts with the support of the Office
of the Governor and the New York State Legislature.

Support for the translation of this book was provided by
Acción Cultural Española, AC/E.

Book design and composition by Mulberry Tree Press, Inc.

Bellevue Literary Press is committed to ecological stewardship in our book
production practices, working to reduce our impact on the natural environment.

♾ This book is printed on acid-free paper.

Manufactured in the United States of America.

First Edition

10   9   8   7   6   5   4   3   2   1

paperback ISBN: 978-1-954276-07-9
ebook ISBN: 978-1-954276-08-6

Perhaps it would be nice to be alternately
victim and executioner.

—Charles Baudelaire

Canción

The Conference

I arrived in Tokyo disguised as an Arab.

At the airport exit, a small delegation from the university was awaiting me, despite its being past midnight. One of the Japanese professors—the hierarch, evidently—was the first to greet me in Arabic, and I simply smiled, in equal parts courtesy and ignorance. A young woman, whom I took to be either the hierarch's assistant or a grad student, wore a white mask and sandals so dainty she looked barefoot; she kept bowing her head to me in silence. Another professor welcomed me, in poor Spanish, to Japan. A younger professor shook my hand and then, still holding it, explained in English that the official chauffeur from their university department would take me to the hotel right away, so I could rest before the event the following morning. The chauffeur, a short gray-haired old man, was dressed as a chauffeur. After recovering my hand and thanking them all in English, I said goodbye—imitating their gestures of reverence— and set out after the old man, who had already picked up speed on the sidewalk and was taking quick, anxious steps in the light drizzle.

In no time we got to the hotel, which was very close to the university. Or at least that's what I thought I understood from the chauffeur, whose English was even worse than my five or six words of Arabic. I also understood him to say that that part of Tokyo was famous for its prostitutes or its cherry trees—it wasn't too clear which, and I was embarrassed to ask. He parked in front of the hotel and, with the engine still running, got out of the car, hurried to open the trunk, dropped my things at the entrance (all, it struck me, with the desperation of someone about to pee in their pants), and left whispering words of farewell or of warning.

I stood on the sidewalk, slightly confused but happy to be there at last, amid the shrieking lights of midnight in Japan. The rain had cleared. The black asphalt gleamed neon. The sky was a huge vault of white clouds. I thought it would do me good to go for a little walk before heading up to the room. Smoke a cigarette. Stretch my legs. Breathe in the jasmine of the still-warm night. But I was afraid of the prostitutes.

I HAD COME TO JAPAN TO PARTICIPATE in a Lebanese writers' conference. After receiving the invitation a few weeks earlier, and after reading it and rereading it until I was sure it wasn't a mistake or a joke, I'd opened the closet to find my Lebanese disguise—among my many disguises—inherited from my paternal grandfather, born in Beirut. I'd never been to Japan before. And I had never been asked to be a Lebanese writer. A Jewish writer, yes. A Guatemalan writer, obviously. A Latin American writer, of course. A Central American writer, less and less. A U.S. writer, more and more. A Spanish writer, when traveling on that passport was desirable. A Polish writer, on one occasion, at a Barcelona bookstore that insisted—insists—on shelving my books in the Polish literature section. A French writer, since I lived for a time in Paris and some people assume I'm still there. I keep each of those disguises on hand, nicely ironed and hanging in the closet. But I'd never been invited to participate in anything as a Lebanese writer. And playing an Arab for a day at a conference at the University of Tokyo seemed a trivial matter if it was going to enable me to see the country.

HE SLEPT IN HIS CHAUFFEUR'S UNIFORM. That's what I thought when I saw him standing beside me, unmoving, undaunted, waiting for me to finish my breakfast so he could drive me to the university. The old man had his hands behind his back, his pompous blank stare fixed on one exact point on the wall before us in the hotel cafeteria. He didn't greet me. He didn't say a word. He didn't rush me. But the whole of him resembled a water balloon about to burst. Nor did I greet him. I simply looked down and kept eating my breakfast as slowly as I could while I read over my notes on a sheet of hotel stationery and practiced, in hushed tones, the various ways of saying thank you in Arabic. Shukran. Shukran lak. Shukran lakum. Shukran jazelan.

Then, when I finished my miso soup, I stood up, smiled at the black-and-white balloon beside me, and went to get some more.

MY LEBANESE GRANDFATHER WASN'T LEBANESE. I began to find this out or to understand it a few years ago, while in New York, searching for clues and documents about his firstborn son, Salomón, who died as a child, not in a lake, as I'd been told when I was growing up, but there, in some private clinic in New York, and was buried in some cemetery in the city. I didn't manage to locate any documents about the boy Salomón (nothing, not one, as if he hadn't died there either, in a private clinic in New York), but I did find the actual logbook, in perfect condition, from the ship that brought my grandfather and his siblings over on June 7, 1917. The ship was called the *Espagne.* It had set sail from Ajaccio, the capital of Corsica, where all of the siblings had gone with their mother after fleeing Beirut (days or weeks before setting off for New York, they'd buried her there, but today nobody knows what my great-grandmother died of, or where on

15

the island her grave is located). My grandfather, as
I read in the ship's logbook, was then sixteen years
old, single, spoke and read French, worked as a shop
assistant (Clerk, typed out) and his nationality was
Syrian (Syrian, also typed out). Next to that, in the
Race or People column, the word Syrian was also
typewritten. But then the immigration officer had
corrected or doubted himself: he crossed the word
out and wrote over it, by hand, the word Lebanese.
And, you see, my grandfather always said he was
Lebanese, I said, the microphone hardly working,
although Lebanon, as a country, was not founded
until 1920, three years after he and his siblings left
Beirut. Prior to that, Beirut was part of Syrian territory. Legally, they were Syrians. They'd been born
Syrians. But they called themselves Lebanese. Perhaps as their race or people, the way it was written
in the logbook. Perhaps as their identity. And so I
am the grandson of a Lebanese man who was not
Lebanese, I told the audience at the University of
Tokyo, and dropped the microphone. I don't know
whether out of respect or confusion, the Japanese
audience remained silent.

The Bedouin

My grandparents lived in a palace. To me, at least, it was a palace. They used to say that my Lebanese grandfather, on a long trip through Mexico in the mid-forties, had fallen in love with a house and then had its same Mexican architect come to Guatemala, with the same rolled-up blueprints under his arm, to build him the same house on some land he'd recently purchased on Avenida Reforma. I don't know if the story is true. Probably not, or not so much. Doesn't really matter. Every house has its story, and every house, to someone, is a palace.

I remember its smell. Each morning, a short, testy housekeeper named Araceli would work her way through the whole house—the huge foyer, the three living rooms, the two dining rooms and two studies, the billiard room, and the six bedrooms on the second floor—carrying a censer filled with eucalyptus leaves. My brother and I were afraid of this old woman, who was our height, had gray hair, wore a black uniform, and yelled a lot, and who always seemed to emerge like a ghost from a cloud of white smoke. It's impossible to forget the effect that that daily dose of eucalyptus had, over the course of decades, on the walls and the wood floors and the Persian rugs that my grandfather had brought from Beirut. But the house didn't smell only of eucalyptus. The aroma was far more complex, far more elegant, comprised also of all the fragrances and spices that emanated like souls from the kitchen. And the kitchen was the territory of Berta, the cook my Egyptian grandmother had stolen from a Guatemalan restaurant called El Gran Pavo, and whom she'd later trained in the art of Arabic cuisine and the art of Israeli cuisine (while surely there is one, I was lucky never to have known the difference). There they fried falafel and kibbe. They baked bagels, pita bread, sambouseks filled with cheese, with spinach, with eggplant. They made mujaddara (jaddara, my grandfather called it), an exquisite dish of rice and lentils served with fried onion and a yogurt, cucumber, and mint sauce. They made yapraks: grape leaves stuffed with rice, lamb, pine nuts, and tamarind. They prepared, on very special occasions, a Sephardic stew, boiled long and slow (twenty-four hours), called hamin. They made fresh yogurt, and various cheeses and jams. In the pantry there were always jars filled with anise pastries, trays of baklava diamonds, a few wooden barrels filled with the olives (black, purple, green) that my grandfather imported from Lebanon. But, in the kitchen, Berta also returned to her Guatemalan roots, and made shredded beef hilachas and chicken jocón and tamales and pepián and kak'ik and a miraculously thick corn atol. And there, too, every night, in a small copper pot, she made my grandfather his Turkish coffee with toasted cardamom seeds, since he needed a cup of Turkish coffee to get to sleep.

My grandfather sat at the head of the dining room table, the copper pot in his hand, pinkie slightly raised (his three-carat diamond ring twinkling), serving everyone a small cup of Turkish coffee, whether they wanted it or not. He took loud, crude slurps. He shouted if it wasn't boiling hot. At my grandparents' house, Turkish coffee was much more than coffee: it was a rite, a cadence, a spell, an end point to things both sweet and bitter, the last of which coincided with a visit from an Argentine cousin named Berenice.

THIS IS YOUR COUSIN BERENICE.

I was kneeling on the Persian rug in the foyer, stacking my grandmother's poker chips into towers. Right above me sparkled the enormous candelabra, which I always thought was made of diamonds and which required a complicated system of cranks and pulleys to be cleaned. It was nighttime. I was embarrassed to be in my pajamas and slippers.

Come now, children, say hello, someone said, and they left us alone together.

I stacked another chip. The red tower collapsed.

All the same color?

Berenice sat down in front of me. In her mouth, a black hole in place of two or three incisors. She had the blondest hair I'd ever seen—it was almost silver. She wore an airy pink dress. Her knees were all scratched up.

I said do the towers have to be all the same color?

I don't know, I managed to stammer.

Hierarchy was quickly established. I had yet to lose a single tooth.

Better if you mix the colors, she said.

The adults were drinking and chatting in the living room as wheezing and snoring from the second floor seemed to rain down upon us.

What's that?, she asked, forehead creased, eyes cast upward. That, I said, is Nono.

BERENICE HAD COME FROM BUENOS AIRES with her parents to visit Nono. That was what we called him, Nono, the husband of one of my grandmother's sisters, an old man with white hair and slow, kindly gestures. I remember four things about him. One: he was a faithful devotee of cowboy movies. Two: he was born in Salonica, Greece, and whenever someone sneezed, he would say in his native Ladino, Bivas, kreskas, engrandeskas, komo

21

un peshiko en aguas freskas, amen. Which was something like: You're born, you grow, you thrive, you dream, like a fishie in the stream. Three: he had fled Paris with one of my grandmother's sisters just after their wedding, a few days before the German occupation, leaving the apartment they'd bought on Rue de Vaugirard furnished but unlived in. And four: one day he just showed up prostrate on a white cot in the second-floor hallway at my grandparents' house.

I never understood why this old man moved to my grandparents' house, or why they put him there, out in the hallway, and not in one of the six unoccupied bedrooms. But suddenly there he was: very ill, gaunt, always accompanied by a nurse and always in a white gown, muttering incoherently and lying faceup on the cot they'd placed at the end of the second-floor hallway—in front of three big picture windows—that circled the entire second floor and had an iron railing that overlooked the enormous foyer at the entrance.

That was when relatives started coming from other countries to visit him. And that was when Nono's wheezing and snoring began to thunder through the house like a perpetual storm.

BETTER LIKE THIS, SHE WHISPERED.

Berenice's long fingers continued to dismantle my blue, black, and yellow towers and then form new ones, calmly, skillfully, combining the poker chips. She was focused. From within the black hole of her smile poked a little tip of tongue.

What're you looking at?

Nothing.

Oh, nothing, sure.

I'm not, I'm not looking at anything.

You're looking at something.

I kept quiet and Berenice kept stacking chips, slowly, carefully.

Later, she said, I'll show you my tushie.

THE STAIRS AT MY GRANDPARENTS' HOUSE were magnificent.

Go up two, she said, then down one. Like this.

A burgundy-colored rug led up the stairs to a sort of landing.

Now, she said, stay there.

I obeyed and stopped on the landing, where the stairs bifurcated and you had to decide whether to climb the rest of the way up on the left or the right, that is, to the three bedrooms on the left or the three bedrooms on the right (though there was just one wide hallway, which circled the entire second floor).

Now, she said, get under there.

On the landing, there was a cedar side table with fresh-cut roses and a set of bronze scales and framed photos—in case, I imagined, you had trouble deciding whether to keep going on the right or on the left and wanted to just land there for a bit first, on the landing.

Boy, are they ugly, she said, looking up.

Above the small cedar table, high on the wall, hung a grandiose wrought-iron relief of two whinnying horses, a design my grandfather had copied from a highball glass.

I'll hide here, she said, with you.

We didn't fit under the cedar table.

When I count to three, Berenice said, you run up the right and I'll run up the left and whoever gets there first and touches Nono wins. Ready?

She counted to three. I let her win. You couldn't pay me to touch Nono.

Us KIDS WERE HAVING DINNER at the kids' table, in the pantry, and the adults in the dining room, just beside it. From time to time, Berta would come in from the kitchen with a tray of just-fried kibbe, with more lemon wedges, with more tahini, with another pitcher of horchata or cinnamon water. Berenice had moved my brother from his spot so she could sit next to me, and spent the whole time talking about her girlfriends in Buenos Aires, her apartment in Buenos Aires, her two cats in Buenos Aires. When dessert was served, my father poked his head into the pantry and announced that we should come into the dining room, quick, because Uncle Salomón was about to read the Turkish coffee.

Read the what?, Berenice asked, grabbing my forearm tightly as all the cousins pushed back their chairs and ran off screaming.

The Turkish coffee, I told her.

How do you read that?

Berenice was still sitting there, still holding on to my forearm.

I explained that first someone drank a small cup of Turkish coffee, and then Uncle Salomón took the small cup and sat looking at the grounds at the bottom and told the person about their future.

No way, she said, letting go of my arm.

It's true.

Berenice opened her eyes wider.

So has he read your coffee?

It only works with grown-ups.

I want him to read my coffee, she exclaimed.

But you're not grown-up.

Just about, she said defensively.

Berenice was already on her feet and walking quickly toward the dining room and so I also raced off, more for her, of course, than for the spectacle of Uncle Salomón and the Turkish coffee.

Uncle Salomón was not my uncle. He was one of my grandmother's cousins. But we all called him Uncle Salomón anyway. He was a tall, thin old man, balding, with a gruff voice, light blue eyes, and the face of a Bedouin. He was always impeccably dressed: jacket and tie and gold cuff links and loafers so shiny they looked new. He was the only person who regularly beat my grandfather at backgammon, on the huge mother-of-pearl and polished shell table that opened up and out like origami. He could conjure small coins from my ear and cigarettes from my nose. He introduced me to my first naked ladies, on playing cards he slipped me in secret. I don't know why, possibly out of a sense of balance or symmetry, I liked knowing that he and his brother had married two sisters.

Have you drunk it all, my dear?, he asked.

Berenice's mother wiped her lips, made an apologetic face, and said yes, almost, all but the dregs.

At the bottom of your cup, he told her, is one-sixtieth of the coffee.

What do you mean, one-sixtieth?, she asked.

Uncle Salomón squinted a bit and furrowed his brow and said that, according to rabbinical commentary on the Talmud, fire is one-sixtieth of hell, and honey is one-sixtieth of manna, and Shabbat is one-sixtieth of the world to come, and sleep is one-sixtieth of death, and dreams are one-sixtieth of prophecy.

Right, she said.

From her tone, it seemed to me that Berenice's mother was unfamiliar with or maybe disdainful of Uncle Salomón's manner of speech, both paradoxical and parabolical.

Now, my dear, place the saucer on top of your cup, but turn it over, upside down.

The dining room had filled with children and adults. Most of us stood close to Uncle Salomón.

Good, he said. Now lift the cup and saucer and, slowly, carefully, spin the cup three times to the left. That is to say, counterclockwise.

There was silence. Berenice's mother, smiling nervously and counting out loud, spun the small cup three times, while Nono made his presence known from his cot on the second floor.

Very good, Uncle Salomón said. Now, still taking care, still holding the cup in your right hand, place your left on top of the saucer. That's right. And finally, in one quick move, I want you to turn the whole thing upside down.

What do you mean, turn the whole thing upside down? The cup and saucer both?

That's right, both. So the cup is facedown on

top of the saucer. Without dripping or spilling anything, do you understand?

Yes, yes, she said, and managed to flip the small cup and saucer without spilling any.

Somebody clapped.

We're finished now, dear, you can leave it all on the table, Uncle Salomón whispered calmly, pulling a small white pack from inside his suede jacket. And now a cigarette, he said, while we wait for the coffee grounds to dry and settle and tell us something.

FOOTSTEPS. THAT WAS THE FIRST THING. We heard their footsteps on the wood floor long before we saw them standing in the dining room doorway. Serious, mustachioed, in their tight khaki uniforms.

The man of the house, one of the soldiers proclaimed: an order more than a question.

I think none of us had heard the doorbell, or seen Araceli cross the dining room to the front door to let them in.

My grandfather stood up. He walked toward them. I remember they did not greet one another, did not shake hands. The same soldier who'd spoken turned and walked out of the dining room, with my grandfather trailing after him. Shortly thereafter we heard the creak of the study door closing.

One of the soldiers followed Araceli to the kitchen, another two went to guard the foyer and front door, and two more remained where they were, staring at us in silence. My father tried to stand.

Remain seated, señor, said one of them.

I just wanted to see if they need anything in the study.

You sit, do you hear me?, he said with one hand on his revolver. They don't need anything.

Someone was outside, on the back lawn. I turned to the picture window overlooking the garden (my grandfather's favorite place to go for a secret smoke), and in the darkness saw an even darker shadow holding a dark rifle.

Would you like anything to drink, officers? Some coffee?, my grandmother asked demurely, maybe just to break the silence, but neither one replied.

Suddenly somebody threw something or broke something in the kitchen. We heard strange shouting coming from the study. We heard banging and wheezing and snoring on the second floor.

What's that?

I didn't know at what point Berenice had grabbed my hand.

It's a nurse, upstairs, taking care of my husband, said Nono's wife, with a slight tremor to her voice.

The soldier, looking up at the second-floor hallway, lit a cigarette.

I hope that's what it is, señora, and not something else, he said all smokily.

I'll go check, she whispered.

You will not go anywhere, señora, the man spat, then whispered something to the other soldier, who sped out of the dining room and up the stairs, and I pictured him on the landing, looking at the photos and the fresh-cut flowers and the two wrought-iron horses.

The first soldier stood there, pawing the bronze mezuzah nailed to the doorframe. One of my aunts told him it was a Jewish talisman, that it was called a mezuzah, that it contained a scroll of parchment with verses from the Torah, that people put them there, on the doorframes of their homes, to bring good luck.

The soldier went on struggling with it, banging it with his fist, as though he wanted to remove it from the doorframe and take it with him so that he, too, could have good luck.

Nobody said a word. Nobody moved. The adults were attempting to calm the children, stroking them and whispering to them, while also attempting to determine what was going on, what so many soldiers wanted with my grandfather, whose were the strident, intrusive voices we now heard coming from all over the house. Some from the huge foyer. Others, more muted, from the study. Others mixed in with wheezing from the stairs and second floor. Others from the kitchen or the backyard. I remember thinking that I wanted to be deaf. I wanted to put my fingers in my ears and be deaf and so not have to hear those voices that I, in a very childlike way, understood were not entirely good, were out of place, did not belong to my world of eucalyptus and baklava and colored poker chips. Suddenly my grandparents' enormous house was too small. I let go of Berenice's hand.

Look, she whispered, elbowing me.

Uncle Salomón was reading the coffee.

At some point, Uncle Salomón had leaned over the table and taken the coffee cup and the saucer and was now studying the various shapes and shadows in the dried grounds. We all just watched him in silence (except for the soldier, who was still smoking in the dining room doorway and had no idea what Uncle Salomón was doing). We watched him maneuver the cup and rotate the saucer and raise his eyebrows and shake his head and sigh gently and even half smile. And we all half smiled as well, or tried to half smile, or at least calmed down a bit. But Uncle Salomón didn't say a thing. He never said a thing. He was never willing to say what he read in those grounds, or to say why he never again agreed to read another cup of Turkish coffee. Some of the family thought he'd seen Nono's impending death. Others, that he'd seen Berenice and her parents' hasty return to Buenos Aires. Others, that he'd seen the reflection of the present, of that moment, of all those soldiers prowling through the house like wild beasts while one of them—I would learn decades later— was in the study, informing my grandfather of the final whereabouts of one of the men who had kidnapped him in January of 1967. But we never found out: Uncle Salomón never said a thing. He simply finished reading that last Turkish coffee and placed the small cup and saucer on the table and lit another cigarette as though nothing had happened, half smiling, half smoking, half smirking at something with the whole of his Bedouin face.

Beni

I wanted to ask him if he'd really had to eat his own dog. But the question seemed almost unutterable, so I just fastened my seat belt and started to feel queasy from the mental image of his dismembered dog, or perhaps from the jerky way he was driving the white delivery van. Outside, the city was suddenly another city.

And do you like living up there, in the United States?

I was making an effort to keep my eyes on the road so that I wouldn't feel any sicker, but I couldn't stop glancing at his hands on the wheel—hands that were too pale and delicate and small, I thought, to have done everything they allegedly did.

I told him I did, I liked it. Although I knew his question wasn't a question, but a judgment.

We were driving through a slum in the capital. All the buildings had an unfinished look about them: brick and concrete walls, corrugated metal roofs, columns with rebar still sticking out, windows with broken glass or no glass at all. The asphalt on the road was full of holes; he didn't even bother to swerve.

Burned rubber, he said.

I'd noticed the same smell, and also a faint black cloud hovering in the air. But I didn't know what it was.

Protesters nearby, he said, burning tires. There's a rag and a bottle of vinegar in the glove compartment, if the smell bothers you.

We stopped at a red light. On one corner, an old indigenous man was down on his knees, his clothes tattered, his hand outstretched. On the other corner, two young men who looked like gang members were staring at us, or possibly they were just staring at the white delivery van. I felt a strong urge to close my window and lock the door. But I remembered the gun that he always carried with him, tucked beneath his brown poly-ester blazer.

And are you working over there?, he asked as he used his hand to wipe the sweat from his forehead. I could've told him no, I wasn't, that I'd recently finished my first semester of engineering at the university. But I remained silent. And he didn't ask any more.

We stopped in front of a huge green gate. There was a security hut on one side, painted the same shade of musty green. Above it hung a flag, lifeless, like an old rag, white and blue.

I left for the United States once, too, he said.

He reached out one of his small hands, grabbed a pack of Rubios from the dashboard, and lit one. I noticed that his forearm had a poorly drawn and blurry tattoo of two jaguars.

Not in an airplane like you, he said as he exhaled a quick burst of smoke to establish the difference between his trip and mine. I was fifteen, he said, and I took off on foot, by myself, with nothing more than a wool rucksack. I managed to get as far as Mapastepec, where two Mexican policemen nabbed me while I was eating tacos. They shoved me into a truck filled with young men and boys, and a few hours later dumped all of us back on this side of the border. And here I've stayed ever since, on my best behavior, and he flashed me his mercury smile.

The gate groaned a little and a young man stuck his head out. When he saw us, he pushed the gate as if in a hurry until it was wide open. We advanced slowly beside the young man—body taut, face expressionless, hand firm to his forehead—who blurted out something terse that I couldn't quite understand. And we entered the military barracks.

You smoke?

He'd asked me that in a whisper as we were walking through an open-air parking lot, past soldiers and military jeeps and trucks with green tents and an antique tank merely for decoration and an all-black German shepherd who never took his eyes off us, his leash tied to the trunk of a cypress tree, his white fangs visible despite the muzzle.

Sometimes, I said.

Near the German shepherd, an old military officer was standing on a small patch of lawn. He wore black boots and a red beret. In his right hand he held a machete.

What do you mean, sometimes?, he asked mockingly.

The old officer suddenly raised the machete and, using the side of the blade, hit a badminton shuttlecock that proceeded to fly through the air, over an invisible net, eventually landing on the other side of the lawn. And the officer, his fist held high, celebrated as if he'd won the point.

Either you smoke or you don't, he said.

The old officer walked over to where the shuttlecock had landed. He picked it up from the ground and once again smacked it with the machete to the other side of the lawn. The dog barked a couple of times as it watched the small projectile soar back over the invisible net and land softly next to the cypress tree. And the officer, waving his machete in the air, once again celebrated the point.

Well, in there, he said, pointing toward the building and offering me the open pack of cigarettes while the officer shouted something and celebrated another point behind us, it's better if you smoke.

I WAS SURPRISED TO SEE THAT THE INSIDE of the Matamoros General Barracks was nothing but a bureaucratic office. There were rows of metal desks and metal chairs and metal-looking soldiers, impeccably dressed and moving with the slow, predictable lethargy of electric mannequins in a shop window. I was also surprised that, despite all the chaos and all the soldiers, there was an unnerving silence. A silence of oscillating fans and muffled voices and clattering typewriters and the occasional ringing of a telephone. A silence that made me think of a recently washed bedsheet flapping in the wind. Perhaps due to all the people smoking, the light was yellowish and hazy—I would later realize that all the windows were obstructed with bars, the panes painted jet black. At the entrance to the hall, withering and abandoned and barely lit, stood a small Christmas tree.

I was walking behind him, smoking, watching him weave between the metal desks with stoic, decisive steps. The soldiers greeted him from their chairs. Most said a few words or made a simple gesture with their chins; a few stood up and shook his hand. None of them greeted me. None of them acknowledged I was there, as if it was forbidden, in that place, even to look at a civilian.

We reached the last desk, at the end of the large hall. A small, slender woman stood up, and I immediately thought that she was far too young to work at a military barracks.

You have everything I asked for?, he asked me discreetly, one of his small warm hands resting on my shoulder, the other stubbing out his cigarette in a pedestal ashtray filled with butts. After also stubbing out my own, I handed him a white envelope, which he quickly stashed in the inside pocket of his brown polyester coat. Good, he said, and this is for you, and he gave me his pack of Rubios. I have another one, he said, letting out a strange cackle that I initially judged ironic, then perverse. You stay here with the young lady, he said, and he walked down a long dark hallway to a black door and opened it without knocking and finally closed it behind him.

Sit down, she said in her bagpipe voice.

Everyone called him Beni. I always knew him as Beni. Not too long ago, however, I came across his obituary in the newspaper and learned that his name had been Benito Cáceres Domínguez. Or let's just say that was his name. Here, for security reasons, that'll be his name.

I can't recall if he'd been an employee of my Lebanese grandfather's, or he'd been an employee of my father's, or he hadn't been an employee of either of them and they'd both just hired him from time to time to help out with certain official paperwork and procedures. I rarely saw him and didn't know too much about him except that he always dressed in a white button-down shirt and a brown polyester blazer, and that he always drove around in a beat-up white delivery van, and that he always had a gun tucked in a holster under his left arm. As a kid, I was convinced I'd seen Beni for the first time one night when he prowled around my grandfather's house with a group of soldiers while my uncle Salomón was reading coffee grounds and one of the soldiers was talking to my grandfather in the privacy of his study. But later, as a teenager, my father would tell me emphatically—too emphatically, it occurred to me then or it occurs to me now—that

Beni had never been there that night. Beni, before, he said, had been a Kaibil. When I asked him what a Kaibil was, my father said a soldier. But given his expression, or perhaps given his insistent yet nervous tone, I understood at once that a Kaibil was more than just a soldier.

THE KAIBILES, I WOULD COME TO LEARN, are the elite commando forces of the Guatemalan army, highly trained, starting in the early 1970s, in the midst of the civil war, in counterinsurgency tactics and jungle warfare. They take their name from the Mayan prince and warrior Kaibil Balam (he who has the strength and astuteness of two jaguars, in the Mam dialect), who had to undergo a series of trials before receiving the title of heir to the throne; afterward (due to that same strength and astuteness of two jaguars) he was never captured in the jungle by the Spanish conquistadors.

The Kaibiles' training is both legend and nightmare.

It takes place over sixty days at a hamlet deep inside the tropical jungle of Petén called the Inferno (a sign over the entrance warns the young cadets of what's to come: BIENVENIDOS AL INFIERNO). Besides the usual training in extreme combat and torture techniques for extracting information from rebels, the recruits are subjected to a series of trials designed to be both psychologically demeaning and a test of their supposedly unwavering trust. Like throwing themselves blindfolded from a bridge or a helicopter. Like being awakened every hour through the night, or not being allowed to sleep at all for several nights in a row. Their only daily meal—a meager serving of black beans and rice—must be consumed with their hands in less than three minutes. Hunger, methodically imposed, is devastating. A hunger that reaches its extreme during their final trial, formally or informally named the Dismembering of the Mascot: the recruit must spend two weeks on an inhospitable deserted island, where he'll have to use all of his skills in order to survive. His sole companion on the island will be a puppy, one he'd received at the start of his training and that he'd cared for and nurtured over those sixty days, and which now, on the island, he'll have to slaughter and skin and dismember with a machete or with his own teeth and drink its blood and eat its raw meat in order to survive and officially become not only a Kaibil but also—as per the ninth commandment of the Decalogue of the Kaibiles—a killing machine.

THE YOUNG WOMAN HADN'T ONCE stopped typing with her little-girl fingers. Several times I thought about saying or asking something—anything not to feel abandoned—but she looked so focused that I didn't want to interrupt her. Soldiers would walk over and leave papers and files on her desk without her even glancing up. Other soldiers were still going in and out the black door at the end of the hallway. Meanwhile, I just kept smoking, perhaps because I had nothing else to do, or because Beni had warned me that in there it was better if I smoked. In any case, I was only getting more and more anxious. What if it wasn't a simple bureaucratic procedure, as my father had told me the previous day at the cemetery?

WE WERE STANDING AT THE GRAVE of my Lebanese grandfather, who had died of a heart attack while I was finishing my first semester at the university. And now, more than thirty days later, as dictated by Jewish tradition, we were finally allowed to lay the headstone. A massive rectangular white marble headstone, with my grandfather's name chiseled and painted in black, which was also my name chiseled and painted in black.

It's a simple bureaucratic procedure, my father whispered to me as the rabbi chanted some Jewish prayer under a light drizzle, surrounded by my family members dressed in black raincoats and standing under black umbrellas. It doesn't mean anything, my father whispered. And it's also your duty. Whether you like it or not, whether you live in Guatemala or not, you're still a Guatemalan, and every Guatemalan man who turns eighteen has to enlist in the military and receive his official military ID card. That's the law, he declared with authority, and didn't say anything else, and so I just listened to the rabbi pray in an incomprehensible Hebrew and stared at my name chiseled and painted in black and thought that in some way it was also my headstone.

I WAS STRUCK BY THE SILENCE.

The young lady had stopped tapping keys for the first time and was now placing a red velvet cloth over the old typewriter with the loving care of a mother tucking in her sleepy child. Then, after picking up all the papers and files from her desk and sticking them inside a drawer that she proceeded to lock, she began putting on an endless series of sweaters and sweatshirts and jackets. First a light turquoise-colored sweater, then a gray sweater with small buttons, then a navy blue wool sweater, then a white sweatshirt, then a white sweatshirt with a hood, then a heavy winter jacket, then a long beige raincoat. I stared at her, a bit confused, since the heat was unbearable both inside and outside the barracks. It occurred to me that she might have been sick, maybe had a fever, maybe something much worse. But I didn't get a chance to ask. As I watched her stand up and turn off a table lamp and grab her small handbag, I finally realized that it was five in the afternoon and she was leaving for the day, and that all the other employees were also putting their things away and leaving for the day, and that I would be left there by myself, in the middle of a dreary, empty military barracks. And so I also stood up in order for her at least to acknowledge my presence, and I heard a voice very similar to my own—though an octave higher—asking her in a stammer whether I should stay there, whether it would be much longer, whether it was, in fact, just a simple bureaucratic procedure.

She stood still and shot me a glance filled with something that might have been disdain or mercy.

I couldn't say, she said, then turned and left.

I sat down again in the chair. I lit my last cigarette as one by one the overhead bulbs turned off. In the distance, at the other end of an already darkened barracks, the red and green Christmas lights were still flickering.

THE FIFTY-EIGHT KAIBILES WEREN'T DRESSED as Kaibiles. That same afternoon, while they were getting ready, they'd received an order from their commanding officers to disguise themselves as guerrilla fighters: olive green T-shirts, red armbands, jeans.

They'd also been ordered to leave behind their military weapons (Galil shotguns and M16s) and only take weapons typically used by the guerrillas (old rifles and handguns). At nine o'clock on the night of December 5, 1982, the fifty-eight Kaibiles climbed into two nonmilitary trucks and left the air base at Santa Elena, Petén. They drove for over two hours in torrential rain, until they reached the entrance to a dirt road. It was almost midnight. The Kaibiles got out of the two trucks—which they would abandon there—and started the six-kilometer walk through the jungle. Another man led them through the darkness in silence. He was barefoot. His indigenous clothes were all torn. His hands were tied behind his back and there was a noose around his neck. Finally, at two-thirty in the morning, the Kaibiles reached the small village. It was still raining. They split up into groups of three and four and started going shack by shack, yelling, knocking down doors, until they'd woken up the more than fifty families. They put all the men inside the small schoolhouse made of guano. The women and children were put inside the two churches, one Catholic, the other Evangelical. The Kaibiles demanded to know where they were hiding the nineteen rifles.

None of the villagers understood. They didn't know that two months earlier, in an ambush not far from there, the guerrillas had killed twenty-one soldiers and stolen nineteen rifles. Now the military government believed that those nineteen rifles were hidden in that small village lost somewhere in the tropical jungle, and that its residents were guerrilla sympathizers. Red area, they called it. At six in the morning, then, with the first light of day just breaking, after informing their commanding officers by radio that they'd found no rifles nor communists nor communist propaganda nor guerrillas, the fifty-eight Kaibiles received their final order: Vaccinate them all.

IT WAS NIGHTTIME. OR MAYBE NOT. Impossible to know for sure with the windows painted black. The hands of time, I began to understand, don't tick at the same pace inside a military barracks.

Sitting there in the dark, my fear and anxiety only grew every time I pondered the absurd idea of getting up and walking through the labyrinth of desks to search for a way out. But out where? And how? And what if the old officer was still on the lawn playing badminton with his machete? What if a soldier stopped me and asked me who I was and what I was doing there so late at night? I didn't even have any ID with me; I'd given my papers to Beni in the white envelope, along with some dollars. No, it was better not to move, to wait right there. The only thing that gave me a slight sense of refuge was the chair itself, and I clung to it both physically and mentally (I didn't notice or didn't care about the pain in my hands, which had too long been clutching the seat). From the chair I saw the silhouette of a cleaning woman sweeping the floor of the entire hall, then mopping the floor of the entire hall, then emptying out each small trash can. From the chair I saw the shadows of soldiers as they hurried between the desks, always ignoring me. And from the chair I kept staring hopefully at the black door at the end of the hallway, even though it had been a while since anyone had gone in or come out.

I closed my eyes, but I couldn't say if it was because of the anxiety or exhaustion I was feeling, or simply because I no longer wanted to see anything. I had a strange taste in my mouth, which could have just been the taste of too many cheap cigarettes, although it could also have been the taste of defeat. I took a deep breath and had even started to relax a little, when out of nowhere I thought I heard tormented moans, like those of a dying animal. And for the first time I wondered if somewhere deep inside the barracks there weren't prison cells and prisoners. Perhaps in the basement. Or upstairs, on the second floor. Or on the other side of the black door at the end of the hallway. These were the last days of 1989 and the country was still in the midst of the civil war and it wasn't implausible to think that somewhere inside—above or below or behind me—there were prisoners of war. The barracks, at that very moment, ceased to be an ordinary bureaucratic office, and I decided that it was better not to close my eyes so I wouldn't have to hear any suffering or imagine any prisoners lying on the floor of a dark, damp cell. And feeling exasperated, as if on the brink of something, I remembered the frog that my physics professor had told us about a few weeks earlier, to illustrate a concept of thermodynamics.

There were around two hundred first-year students sitting in a huge auditorium, almost all of us half-asleep due to hangovers or boredom or both,

when the old professor started talking about the
boiled frog theory. He told us that if you drop a
frog into a pot of boiling water, the frog will jump
right out and save itself. But if you place a frog
into a pot of lukewarm water and then proceed
to gradually turn up the burner, the frog won't
notice the slight increases in temperature and
will eventually be boiled in the pot (the entire
auditorium gasped in unison). But the professor
quickly and theatrically raised a hand, as if to say
stop everything, and then explained that it was
a myth, that the boiled frog theory, according to
scientists, was incorrect. Back in the nineteenth
century, he said, German physiologist Friedrich
Goltz, while conducting experiments to identify
the exact location of the soul, demonstrated that
as soon as the temperature reached twenty-five
degrees Celsius, the frog would immediately jump
out of the pot. Because the frog is an amphibian,
he explained, which self-regulates body temperature by constantly moving about. Thermoregulation, it's called. And so, he said, if it can, a frog
will always jump out of the pot. Some students
giggled. Others sighed. I didn't see the point. And
I'm sure no one else there did, either. He was now

standing with his back to us, scribbling on the blackboard the formula for the first law of thermodynamics ($\Delta u = q - w$, which states that the amount of energy in the universe is neither created nor destroyed, but remains constant), right next to a poorly sketched smiling frog.

And sitting there in the dark of a military barracks, I thought: I'm the frog. I thought: This chair is the pot. I thought: A gigantic military hand is turning the knob to increase the temperature of the water. I thought: They want to boil me alive. I thought: I'm being boiled alive. I thought: Eduardo Halfon, chiseled and painted in black. I thought: The German scientist Friedrich Goltz never found the exact location of the soul but did prove the boiled frog theory incorrect. I thought: Thermoregulation. I thought: I have to jump.

And so I jumped from the chair and ran the twenty or thirty steps to the black door at the end of the hallway and started banging on it with my fist as if my own existence depended on it, and the door slowly creaked open.

A THREE-MONTH-OLD BABY WAS DROPPED alive into a dry well. It was noon. The fifty-eight Kaibiles headed for the two churches and took out all the children and put them in a straight line and told them not to worry, that they were only being vaccinated. The older ones received a blow to the head with a sledgehammer or a gunshot to the temple and were then pushed into the well. The younger ones needed only to be held by their feet and smashed against a wall or against the trunk of a tree and then dropped into the well. The girls and women, before falling dead or half-dead into the well, were raped. Next came the men. One by one, kneeling and blindfolded, they were interrogated and tortured and beaten and shot and then dropped into the well. The massacre finally ended at six in the evening. Night fell and still there came sounds of agony and sobbing from the well and a Kaibil dropped in a grenade to silence them. Some of the women in the village had been kept alive— the Kaibiles needed their dinner of black beans and rice. In the morning, another fifteen indigenous men who had been working far away in their maize plantations came back to the village. But the well was already full. So the Kaibiles torched the fifty shacks and the schoolhouse made of guano and the Catholic church and the Evangelical church and then took the fifteen indigenous men with them and also the last remaining women in the village and later, in the deep of the jungle, they shot and slit the throats of them all, except for a young boy who managed to escape by running through the trees, and two girls of fourteen and sixteen, whom they dressed up as guerrillas and kept alive for three days, raping them repeatedly as they made their way across the jungle. They left one girl's body in the bushes, the other hanging from an oak tree.

Years later, forensic anthropologists would recover 162 bodies from the well. The village, named Dos Erres, was now nothing more than overgrown bushes and snakes.

One of the fifty-eight Kaibiles, according to testimony, was Benito Cáceres Domínguez.

A MIDDLE-AGED MAN WAS STANDING on the other side of the black door, one hand still on the knob. His hair was disheveled, his shirt half-open, his face flushed and spotted with tiny droplets of sweat.

He was swaying slightly, as if his plump body was trying to balance itself. His black eyes no longer appeared to be looking at anything.

Here you go, he stammered, his breath reeking of rum, as he handed me a flimsy yet official piece of light blue cardboard.

I don't know why I hadn't recognized him. One possibility is that I wasn't expecting him to open the door himself. Another simpler explanation is that there wasn't enough light in the hallway. But a much more plausible reason is that his physical transformation had gone much further than just having taken off his brown polyester uniform. He was now someone else entirely. His face was someone else's. His body was someone else's. His demeanor was someone else's. His two jaguars were now ferocious and vivid and perfectly tattooed. It was as if when he crossed the threshold of the black door, he'd also crossed another darker and more metaphysical threshold and once again transformed into a Kaibil.

Come in.

There was nothing behind him. Or at least I couldn't make out anything behind him. No people. No noises or moans. No damp prison cells.

I wanted to tell him that I preferred not to go in, that I couldn't go in, that I didn't belong in there, that I'd rather just go back to the chair and wait for him, sitting in the dark. But my mouth couldn't form the words.

Come in, he said again, his voice tart, his eyes like daggers. And this time I understood that it wasn't an invitation. It was a mandate, an order, from one soldier to another.

Canción

They called him Canción because he used to be a butcher. Not because he was a musician. Not because he was a singer (he couldn't even sing). But because when he got out of jail in Puerto Barrios, where he'd been sent for holding up a gas station, he worked for a time in Doña Susana's butcher shop, in a run-down neighborhood in Guatemala City. They say he was a good butcher. Very kind to the ladies from the neighborhood who bought cuts of beef and sausages there. And his nickname, then, stemmed from the alliteration between the words in Spanish for butcher (carnicero) and song (canción). Or at least that's what some of his friends claimed. Others, however, said that he got his nickname thanks to his peculiar, melodic manner of speaking. And still others, perhaps the most intrepid ones, attributed it to his impulsive way of always confessing too much, of singing more than he should. His closest friends, his comrades, called him Ricardo. But his name was Percy. Percy Amílcar Jacobs Fernández. It was he—Percy, or Ricardo, or Canción—who a few years after working as a butcher kidnapped my grandfather.

I GOT THERE TOO EARLY. I walked up to the counter and said hello to the bartender, an elderly gentleman dressed in a white shirt and black pants who had probably been there his entire life, behind that same counter, making drinks for those same clients.

What can I get you, caballero?

I was surprised I'd heard him (he mumbled without opening his mouth, like a ventriloquist), until I noticed that an almost sepulchral silence reigned in the bar. No music. Few patrons. I ordered a Negra Modelo and went to wait for it at the table farthest from a soundless television that hung from the ceiling. At the table next to me, two men were sharing a bottle of rum and a bowl of potato chips;

at another table, an older woman, wearing a mini-skirt and way too much lipstick, was eyeing the newspaper with little or no interest, possibly just looking at the photos; at another table, a man in the sort of coat and tie typically worn by frustrated notaries was using both hands to hold his glass of whiskey, almost clinging to his glass of whiskey, as he observed me with an expression that was serious, indiscreet. I noticed that behind the bar, in an old wooden case with glass doors, were a series of diplomas and gold medals and large silver trophies and a small taxidermied ocelot, about to attack. Far away, at the other end of the bar, were the two swinging doors to the bathrooms: the men's designated by an old magazine cutout of a young and dusty Clint Eastwood, the women's by an old magazine cutout of a loud and busty Marilyn Monroe. Through the large window I could see the silhouettes and lights of the downtown traffic. It was beginning to get dark.

I pulled the small clay ashtray toward me, lit a cigarette, and stared anxiously at the front door, thinking all the while that a bar located on the corner of a round building is surely a metaphor for something.

I WAS BORN ON A DEAD-END STREET. That is, when I was born, in 1971, my parents lived in a new house on a dead-end street. At the top of the street, on Avenida Reforma, there used to be a famous ice-cream parlor on one corner, and a not so famous metal shop on the other. I have no memories of that dead-end street, of course, but several silent home movies serve as evidence of my first years there. Me, as a newborn in my mother's arms, coming home from the hospital in a jade-colored Volvo. Me, as a one-year-old, sitting in a wooden cart painted sky blue while a black goat pulls me up and down the street and an indigenous boy, barefoot and dressed in rags, guides the black goat with a thin lasso (a typical entertainment from that time at wealthier kids' birthday parties). Me, as a two-year-old, spinning in circles in front of the metal shop with tangerine sorbet on my hand and face, and then, in a foreshadowing of many dizzy spells that were to come, throwing up a tangerine stream all over the curb. Me, as a three-year-old, playing with the neighbor's dog, a fat, lazy dachshund named Sancho. And even though there's no silent home movie of it (or perhaps there is), on a cold January morning in 1967, four years before I was born, and while our future house was still under construction, a police car stopping my Lebanese grandfather at the top of the dead-end street, on the corner of Avenida Reforma, to kidnap him.

THE BARTENDER ARRIVED. He placed a Negra Modelo and a huge mug on the table, and I asked him if he couldn't bring me a small glass instead. The old man made a face, one of frustration or maybe bewilderment. So I was forced to explain to him that I like to drink beer slowly, pouring one sip at a time into a small glass, whether it be a tumbler or a goblet or snifter or an old-fashioned. I then thought of telling him to please hurry, since I like to alternate small sips of dark beer with quick drags on my cigarette, although I don't know if it's the bitterness, or superstition. I then thought of telling him (or paraphrasing for him) that the history of my life had become irreparably intertwined with my history of beer and cigarettes. But I remained silent. And the old bartender just made another gesture, only this time a gesture with his entire face, an exaggerated, almost buffoonlike gesture, as if saying yeah, caballero, whatever, but only a madman drinks his beer that way. He snatched the frozen mug from the table and walked back to the counter dragging his feet, and I shuddered as I saw, out of the corner of my eye, that someone had pushed open the front door. Just a boy carrying a flimsy cardboard box. He was selling green parrots.

INSIDE THE POLICE CAR, parked and waiting for my grandfather at the corner of the dead-end street, on that cold morning in January of 1967, were four men. One was half-asleep in the backseat, with a white towel rolled around his neck like a thick scarf. Next to him, another man was cleaning the window with a page of the previous day's newspaper. Another man, the driver, waited in silence, with the engine running, his hands gripping the steering wheel far too tight. And another man was ready to jump out the passenger door the moment he saw the cream-colored Mercedes in the rearview mirror, coming down Avenida Reforma.

Of the four men, only one would survive the civil war.

My grandfather awoke before sunrise. He was anxious (as if he somehow knew what the day held in store for him). He took a shower and dressed slowly, silently, so as not to wake my grandmother. He went down to the dining room and ate breakfast by himself. After making a phone call, he got into his cream-colored Mercedes, started the engine, and drove out through the main gate.

It was still early. The dew and the January cold had not yet lifted. My grandfather got to the bank too soon. It was still closed, and he had to wait outside, standing in the almost deserted street. When it finally opened, my grandfather conducted his business (angrily, the teller would later state) and went back out to his cream-colored Mercedes.

He drove slowly, prudently. Inside one of the front pockets of his trousers was the thick wad of bills he'd just withdrawn from the bank—the equivalent of $2,500—to pay the construction workers their two weeks' salaries. Inside the other front pocket of his trousers was his bankbook, with all of his financial information and current account balance. In his coat's inside pocket were two gold pens. And on his pinkie finger, as always, he was wearing his three-carat diamond ring.

He got to the dead-end street off Avenida Reforma.

There was a police car parked at the top, blocking his way. One of the policemen was already standing on the frontage road and motioned for him to stop and get out of the car.

I WAS POURING MYSELF ANOTHER DRINK of beer into the small glass when someone pushed open the front door and walked into the bar. Just a young guy. He was wearing what looked like a school uniform, but a school uniform late in the day, all disheveled and creased. He walked straight to the older woman in a miniskirt and, after whispering something in her ear that I couldn't quite make out, placed a few bills on the table. It occurred to me that he was there to pay her tab (maybe she was his mother or his grandmother), but she just took the bills without even looking up from the newspaper and stuffed them in her bra. He was still standing beside her, his head bent low, as though he'd been chided, when suddenly someone even younger—a teenager—entered the bar and stood behind him, as though waiting his turn. The first guy ambled out of the bar. Hesitantly, the second guy took a step forward. He also whispered something unintelligible into her ear. He also placed a handful of bills on the table. And the woman, without saying anything, without even looking up, again shoved them into her bra.

TIBURÓN: THE NAME GIVEN by the guerrillas of the Rebel Armed Forces to the police car used on that cold January morning to kidnap my grandfather, or rather, the name given to the car they used as a police car. It had belonged to the government's secretary of information, Baltasar Morales de la Cruz, who had himself been kidnapped a few months earlier (his son, Luis Fernando, was killed in the shoot-out, as was his driver, Chabelo). The guerrillas had arrived in a blue truck to kidnap Morales de la Cruz, but it had stalled in the getaway. So they decided to leave the blue truck behind and take Morales de la Cruz in his own car: a chalk white 1964 Chrysler Imperial Crown. A few months later, that same Chrysler had been painted gray and disguised as a police car—and as a shark—and was lying in wait at the top of the dead-end street to kidnap my grandfather.

THE GUATEMALAN GUERRILLA MOVEMENT was created at the start of the 1960s, in the mountains, by a ghost and a caiman.

On November 13, 1960, about a hundred military officials planned an uprising to combat the imperialist influence of the United States, which secretly, at a private farm called La Helvetia, had been training Cuban exiles and anti-Castro mercenaries for the upcoming Cuban invasion at the Bay of Pigs (at that same private farm, whose owner was a business partner of the Guatemalan president, the CIA had already established a central radio command, from which it would later coordinate the failed invasion). Most of the military officials involved in the uprising were quickly condemned and summarily executed, but two managed to escape into the mountains: a lieutenant named Marco Antonio Yon Sosa and a second lieutenant named Luis Augusto Turcios Lima. Both, as soldiers, had been trained in counterinsurgency tactics by the U.S. Army—one at Fort Benning, Georgia, the other at Fort Gulick, Panama. And while hiding in the mountains, Yon Sosa and Turcios Lima began to organize the country's first guerrilla movement (or front): the Revolutionary Movement 13th November. Just over a year later, in 1962, after a group of soldiers killed eleven university students while they were putting up protest posters in downtown Guatemala City, the Revolutionary Movement 13th November joined forces with the Guatemalan Labor Party to form the Rebel Armed Forces. It's estimated that by the time my grandfather was kidnapped, in January of 1967, there were three hundred guerrilla fighters in the country. Average age: twenty-two. Average time as a guerrilla fighter before getting killed: three years.

Turcios Lima managed to survive in the mountains, his comrades used to say, because he was, in fact, a ghost. Yon Sosa would fool the soldiers at night, his comrades used to say, because he was really a caiman that slept inside the belly of another colossal black caiman. Until the night he was ambushed and killed in Tuxtla, Mexico. And Turcios Lima the ghost showed up one morning in the capital city, charred black in his own burned-out car.

A MIDDLE-AGED MAN STOPPED in the night, on the other side of the glass door. He was dressed entirely in black and staring at each of us sitting inside the bar, as if searching for someone. He then closed his eyes and raised a book high with his right hand. Sinners, he yelled furiously through the glass, his eyes still closed. He yelled something else, a long sentence, possibly a biblical quote that I didn't understand, or that I didn't want to understand, and he fell silent. He was swaying back and forth. He looked as if he was praying wordlessly. Nobody else in the bar seemed to notice him or even acknowledge his presence on the other side of the glass door, and it occurred to me that he, too, came there every night, that he, too, every night, was just another regular at the bar. Suddenly, with the book still held high and his eyes still closed, the man leaned forward and placed his lips to the glass. As if kissing the glass. Or as if kissing all of us sinners inside the bar.

My grandfather got out of his cream-colored Mercedes. He didn't turn off the engine. Didn't shut the door. Didn't even bother to park it properly in the frontage road of Avenida Reforma, outside of the famous ice-cream parlor—it was still early, there were few cars or pedestrians around. The police officer approached, and my grandfather, perhaps because he noticed the policeman's boyish face, or perhaps because he noticed that his uniform was comically large, began speaking to him in an insolent manner. Move that patrol car (index finger in the air). Don't touch me (jerking his arm away). But the officer simply said in a calm voice that he had a warrant for his arrest, for contraband. My grandfather, who spoke loudly and brusquely to everyone, in his heavy Arabic accent,

71

started speaking even more loudly and even more brusquely to the boyish policeman, who didn't want to, or couldn't, give him a clear explanation, and who refused to show my grandfather the supposed arrest warrant. But then the policeman said something to him in a whisper, his words barely a curl of white mist, and my grandfather walked with him to the police car and obediently got into the backseat. And sitting there, between two other policemen, the last thing he saw out of the window was his daughter, my father's eldest sister, racing toward the car. Then everything went black.

THE TWO MEN AT THE TABLE next to mine called the bartender over and ordered another eighth of rum. Their faces were red and sweaty. One of the men, his head bent low, seemed about to fall asleep. The other man was holding an empty bottle in his hands, almost caressing it with sadness or longing. I noticed that there was another empty eighth of rum on the table and thought of asking them why they hadn't just ordered a large bottle to start with, instead of drinking small eighths of a liter, but I decided to guess. Option A: the two men, when they arrived at the bar, planned to drink only an eighth between them, but then, feeling the start of a rum-induced fever, decided to prolong the night and share a second eighth, then a third. Option B: the two men, when they arrived at the bar, had asked the barman for a liter of rum but had been told that unfortunately there were no liter bottles of rum left, just eighths of a liter. Option C: the two men were of the philosophy that rum tastes better in servings of 125 milliliters. Option D: the two men had no philosophy or project whatsoever and simply drank rum with the levity of two blind men standing on the edge of an abyss. And as I was trying to come up with a fifth option to explain drinking rum in that manner, the guy who was about to fall asleep lifted his gaze in my direction—a teary, milky gaze—and spouted: Get the devil out of that fucking thing. It took me a few seconds to realize that he wasn't looking at me or talking to me. The other man, the one who was holding the empty bottle, reached out his other hand and grabbed a lighter from the table and, after igniting it, held the flame to the bottom of the bottle, as though

73

heating it up. Then, carefully, he held the flame to the mouth of the bottle. From the opening there shot out a blue malignant blaze.

MY GRANDFATHER HAD TELEPHONED his eldest daughter that morning, just before leaving the house, to tell her to meet him at the construction site, saying he wanted to show her how the work was going. And so, as she waited there, standing on the dead-end street, she saw from afar how her father had left the cream-colored Mercedes badly parked on the side of Avenida Reforma, the engine still running, the door half-open; how her father yelled and argued with one of the policemen; how that same policeman then whispered something she couldn't hear (she saw only the white mist of the words), but which immediately silenced her father. And without even thinking about it, she had started running down the street, toward them.

Now she was standing in front of the patrol car, defying the policemen, insulting the policemen, shouting at them that she refused to move out of the way until they explained why they were taking her father, why the black hood over his head.

One of the policemen opened his door. He got out slowly. Just as slowly, and smiling slightly, he pointed his machine gun at her.

Move, lady, or I'll rip you in two.

The policeman, impeccably disguised as a policeman, was Canción.

HE HAD THE FACE OF A CHILD. That's what his comrades used to say. That his face was the face of a child. In part due to his large oval eyes. In part due to his skin, so pale and hairless that it appeared to be painted with talcum powder. And in part because he seemed to go through life with a confused expression on his face—his brow furrowed, his gaze opaque and cross-eyed, his mouth agape— an expression of not understanding anything, ever. Although Canción, according to his comrades, understood everything. And his childlike appearance was made even more pronounced by how short he was, or how short he looked to others, when the reality was that his extremities were simply too short for his torso, as if he had the arms and legs of a troll. But despite this childlike appearance, or precisely because of it, Canción never left a party or a bar, according to his comrades, without a woman by his side, clutching his arm. It's not that he was handsome (he was beautiful in the same gentle and androgynous way that a little boy is beautiful), but that he knew how to talk to women. And this, according to some of his comrades, was one of Canción's most peculiar characteristics: his manner of speaking, his way of expressing himself in short, cryptic, almost poetic phrases. He would rarely utter a long or even a complete sentence, and rarely was the meaning of his words in fact their literal meaning. It's not that he spoke in slang, but in his own idiolect. I beheaded a rooster, Canción would say when he'd killed a high-ranking military officer. My armadillo, he would say when referring to his weapon, his machine gun or rifle. Gimme chicharra, he would say when he felt like smoking a cigarette, and gimme quequexque, when he wanted marijuana (as a teenager he'd spent time in prison for drug possession). I dove in or I splashed in, he'd say after visiting one of his two favorite whorehouses, La Locha and La Maruja, named for their respective madams. And this here is my prayer, he'd say with pride and ownership, which meant this here is my prey, my hostage. But Canción's temperament, according to his comrades, maybe as compensation for his boyishness, showed the cold composure of a professional killer or a soldier (which in the end is the same thing). He was relentless. He would never accept less than what had been agreed. Nobody ever saw him give up. Nobody remembers him ever losing with grace. He could be trusted to execute every order, whether bureaucratic or grim or even criminal, without any emotion whatsoever.

OPERACIÓN TOMATE: CODE NAME GIVEN by the guerrillas to the operation of kidnapping my grandfather, due to his skin being so red or pink that to them he looked like a giant tomato.

EL ESPINERO: CODE NAME GIVEN by the guerrillas to the safe house in the Mariscal, a slum on the outskirts of the city, where that cold morning, in January of 1967, they transported and imprisoned my grandfather. On the roof of the small house, on top of a steel and cement tower, a large water tank was clearly visible from a distance, in all directions, from which hung a red lightbulb. When lit, it signaled to guerrilla fighters that there was a prisoner inside.

EL TURCO: CODE NAME GIVEN by the guerrillas to my grandfather during the planning stages of his kidnapping. Though my grandfather wasn't Turkish, he was Lebanese. At that time, in Guatemala, all Jews and Arabs were called Turks regardless of their religion or country of origin. Though of course my grandfather wasn't Lebanese, either. Or not exactly.

I only fully understood or confirmed this not too long ago, while looking for documents at the National Library of Paris, documents from the time my grandfather was living there, at the end of the 1920s, working on Rue du Faubourg-Saint-Honoré.

My grandfather had fled Beirut in 1917, when he was only sixteen years old, with his mother and siblings, at the height of the Great Famine of Mount Lebanon—of the 400,000 inhabitants, more than half would die in less than three years. He lived briefly in New York, in Haiti, in Peru, in Mexico, before getting on a boat that took him back to Europe and arriving in Paris, where he set up a small mercantile business on Rue du Fau-bourg-Saint-Honoré, in partnership with a French Jew by the family name of Gabai. They would buy and sell and ship textiles to his eight brothers, all spread out in several countries in the Ameri-cas (one of his brothers had opened a small fabric shop in Guatemala; my grandfather arrived there in 1930 to help him, met my grandmother, and never left). Société Halfon Gabai, the business was called. Up until a few years ago, in fact, according to family legend, the sign was still there: SOCIÉTÉ HALFON GABAI, in discolored black letters, on the façade of a storefront located on the corner of Rue du Faubourg-Saint-Honoré and Rue de Berri. And that same name, Société Halfon Gabai, was on the

ad I finally found at the bottom of the Annonces
Légales page of a newspaper, after weeks of searching with the help of an old and very kind librarian named Monsieur Patellier. I never knew his
first name, and I never quite understood whether
he worked there or was just a volunteer. Sitting
together at a small table in Salon L, and watching through a huge window as five goats chewed
the garden's weeds (they were brought in by the
library's director, Monsieur Patellier had just told
me, to trim the weeds organically), we read together that, beneath my grandfather's name and date
of birth, it stated in minuscule letters: De nation-
alité syrienne. My grandfather, though he called
himself Lebanese, was legally Syrian, since the
country of Lebanon wasn't established until after
he and his siblings had left Beirut. And that was
that. I thanked Monsieur Patellier, said goodbye
to him and to the five goats, and left satisfied at
having held that sheet of paper from the past in
my hands (as if it were necessary to find and touch
the evidence of this story). But a few days later, I
received a call from the kind librarian, who had
apparently taken my inquiry as a personal chal-
lenge. He told me that he had managed to find

another document, although he didn't specify how or where, which might interest me. I went to meet him that very same night and we again sat at the very same table in Salon L (the five goats in the garden, I supposed, were already sleeping). It was a worn and yellowed photocopy of a certificate from the French government, dated April 26, 1940, authorizing my grandfather's old business partner, Monsieur Gabai, to leave the country. Something very difficult for a Jew to obtain in those years, the librarian explained to me in a whisper that was at once discreet and confused, and I immediately understood or thought I understood that he was speaking from experience, that he'd personally lived through or suffered through something similar during the years of German occupation. The government certificate, however, didn't say anything more. And so holding the yellowed piece of paper in my hands, and also whispering in order not to bother the other readers and researchers in Salon L—although from every wall of the building, as an acoustic solution, hung huge coat of mail tapestries, as if the entire library were a giant medieval knight—I proceeded to tell Monsieur Patellier the rest of the story.

My grandfather, who'd already been living and working in Guatemala for over a decade, had procured a letter of safe conduct for his old French business partner, authorized and signed by General Jorge Ubico, Guatemala's president and dictator since 1931, also known as the Little Napoleon of the Tropics (he liked to dress up and pose like Napoleon), or as Number Five (for the five letters in his first and last names), or as the Hitler of Guatemala (I'm just like Hitler, he used to boast in public). Monsieur Gabai, I explained in my poor French to Monsieur Patellier, managed to get out of Paris just weeks before the German occupation, thanks to a letter of safe conduct that my grandfather had sent him, signed and officially stamped by the Hitler of Guatemala.

YOU GOT ANOTHER ONE OF THOSE.

It took me a moment to realize that the notary, sitting at the next table, was talking to me. His tone was not questioning but demanding. His eyes were turned upward, whether looking at the mossy stains on the ceiling or the soundless

pictures on the television set, I don't know. He
let go of his whiskey, probably for the first time
since I'd arrived, brought two fingers to his lips
and smoked an invisible cigarette, so I'd understand. I said of course, holding out the pack of
Camels and lighter, which he took without a word
but with a slight movement of his chin, perhaps a
gesture of thanks, perhaps no more than a twitch.
I watched as the flame suddenly lit up his greasy,
unshaven face. I accepted the cigarettes and the
lighter back from him and took advantage of the
moment to light another for myself. Won't be
long, he might have murmured in the half gloom
of the bar. Excuse me?, I asked him nervously, but
he just blew a little cloud of grayish smoke toward
the television. It occurred to me that he might
have said I don't belong, or won't be wrong, or be
gone. Then it occurred to me that he might have
said nothing at all and that I might have imagined
it. I made a futile attempt to go back in time a
few seconds and hear his words again. Who won't
be long?, I asked, more nervous still, but he had
already stood up and was walking lethargically
toward Clint Eastwood, cigarette in one hand
and glass of whiskey in the other. Though more

than walking lethargically, he was limping, as if he were injured or very drunk. He leaned forward to push the swinging door with one shoulder and I thought I saw at his side, just beneath his jacket, the metallic black of a gun.

THESE ARE THE RINGLEADERS who seek to foment chaos and anarchy in our country.

That, in big black letters, is what the citizens of Guatemala were told in the headline of a notice that the government distributed and published in newspapers and stuck to the city's lampposts and walls in the final days of September 1968. Beneath the heading are three photos in black and white of three young men, age about twenty. And beneath the three photos, in small letters, it says: With funds contributed by private enterprise and put at the disposal of the government security forces, a reward of ten thousand quetzals is offered to anyone who turns in any of these three criminals or provides information leading to the successful capture of any one of these thugs accused of the assassination of the ambassador of the United

States of America and other recent acts of violence perpetrated in our capital.

The U.S. ambassador was John Gordon Mein. It hadn't been an assassination but a kidnapping attempt that had gone wrong when Mein tried to escape, running down the avenue, where he was quickly riddled with gunfire by the guerrilla fighters. Eight bullet wounds in the back, said the judge after the autopsy. The purpose of the kidnapping had been to exchange the ambassador for the guerrillas' top commander, Comandante Camilo, captured by the army some days earlier. The guerrilla fighters had been waiting for Mein a block from the embassy—he was returning from a lunch—in two rental cars: a green Chevrolet Chevelle (Hertz) and a red Toyota (Avis). Both cars, it was discovered within a few hours, had been rented that same morning by Michèle Firk, a French Jewish journalist and revolutionary who was also Camilo's lover. La Llorona he used to call her, owing to her habit of crying at goodbyes. Ten days after Mein's killing, with the military police about to break down her front door, the journalist and revolutionary Michèle Firk would commit suicide: a gun to the mouth.

One of the three criminals sought in the notice, the one in the middle photo, the one whose expression looked somewhere between sinister and childlike, is Canción. Alias, it says under the photograph, the Butcher.

It's THE LAST DAY OF MARCH 1970. A Tuesday with a hint of spring sunshine. Just past noon. A black Mercedes is driving down Avenida de las Americas, very slowly: for the last week there has been a ban by official decree—due to all the military road-blocks in the city—on driving over thirty kilometers per hour. The driver of the Mercedes is named Edmundo Hernández. Chito, they call him. Sitting in the backseat, reading the paper, is Count Karl von Spreti, the Federal Republic of Germany's ambassador in Guatemala. The driver looks at him in the rearview mirror, a handsome, elegant man, and once again he thinks von Spreti looks like a movie actor—he reminds him of Marcello Mastroianni—and isn't sure when it happened or where they came from, but suddenly two cars are blocking his path in front of the monument to

Christopher Columbus: a white Volkswagen Beetle and a pearl blue Volvo.

Stop, von Spreti orders him, resigned. They've come for me.

Six guerrillas get out of the cars. They have balaclavas and Thompson machine guns (Tommies, they call them). One of the six opens the back door of the Mercedes, takes the count by the arm, and without a word, and meeting no resistance, leads him to the pearl blue Volvo. The guerilla is Canción.

The main purpose of the kidnapping: the exchange of the ambassador for seventeen political prisoners. But the military government, within four days, and by way of a response to the guerrillas' demand, murders two of those they are holding.

That Sunday, somebody uses a pay phone to make a call to the fire station. An anonymous voice tells the fireman on duty that von Spreti is in a low, roofless adobe house at kilometer sixteen of the road to San Pedro Ayampuc, a town on the outskirts of the capital. The firemen head over right away.

They find von Spreti's body in the backyard,

with a single bullet hole in his left breast, a 9mm caliber. The count is sitting on the ground, legs stretched out in front of him, leaning against some bushes. He is still dressed in a fine blue Dacron jacket and a black silk tie. He is holding his glasses in his right hand, as though he had taken them off before dying, right before the shot was fired, so as not to have to see the face of his killer, or so as not to have to see the face of death.

THE BAR DOOR OPENED AND I was disappointed to see a short, dark man walk in. He wore a long blue polyester coat, which was dirty and torn, a palm-straw hat, and a pair of leather and rubber sandals. He was walking slowly, with the help of a cane, or with the help of what I had initially thought was a cane but which turned out to be a bundle of dry twigs tied together with a shoelace. The old man swept the floor a bit before approaching one of the customers with his hand outstretched and mumbling a few unintelligible words, then swept a little more. We all ignored him. He headed toward the dusty face of Clint Eastwood and tried to push the door—I don't know if he was hoping to find the notary in there to also ask him for charity— but it was still locked. He walked back to the glass door and left.

I could still see him through the window for a few minutes: sweeping the sidewalk, holding out his hand in the night, murmuring words in a language nobody else in the world could now understand.

HE'D BEEN KIDNAPPED BY A BEAUTY QUEEN. That's what my grandfather said. At El Espinero, he said, the dark safe house where he was held, there was a beautiful woman who would come and go along with all the other guerrillas, a refined, intelligent woman who always treated him with respect. He never knew her name, but he was convinced she was Rogelia Cruz.

LA ROGE. THAT'S WHAT ROGELIA CRUZ'S friends and relatives used to call her. In 1958, when she was seventeen, while she was completing her studies to be a primary school teacher at the Instituto Normal de Señoritas Belén, she was elected Miss Guatemala. The following summer she traveled to Long Beach, California—her first and only trip abroad—to take part in the Miss Universe pageant. She did not win. But when delivering her speech, wearing typical Mayan dress, she criticized the U.S. government for their intervention in Guatemala in June 1954, when they had orchestrated and financed the toppling of president Jacobo Arbenz, only the second democratically elected president in the country's history.

ARBENZ, OR EL CHELÓN, OR EL SUIZO, insisted in his inaugural address that the reigning economic system in Guatemala was feudal, and in 1952 he began to implement his agrarian reform law, known as Decree 900, whose basic aim—as it stated—was to develop the capitalist economy of the campesinos. Campesinos who had been decimated by poverty and famine (according to that year's census, 57 percent possessed no land of their own; 67 percent died before turning twenty). The first measure in the agrarian reform: abolish the feudal system that operated in the countryside (all forms of serfdom are abolished, it said, and consequently so is obligatory unpaid military service by the campesinos). And the second measure: allow the expropriation of uncultivated lands— that is, the unproductive ones—in exchange for compensation in bonds, in order to redistribute these properties among the poor and the needy, the indigenous and the campesinos. In 1953, Arbenz expropriated almost half of the uncultivated land held by one of the largest landowners, the United Fruit Company (though they owned more than half the arable land in the country, they had planted on less than 3 percent of it), land that the U.S. company had received for free in 1901, as a gift from president and dictator Manuel Estrada Cabrera. Via the Dulles brothers (both brothers, John Foster Dulles, then secretary of state, and Allen Dulles, then director of the CIA, had been lawyers for the company and were at the time on its board of directors), United Fruit put pressure on the Eisenhower administration and Arbenz was rapidly overthrown in a CIA operation called Operation PBSuccess, launching the country into a series of repressive governments and military presidents and genocidal military men and almost four decades of civil war (while John Foster Dulles, in 1955, was named *Time* magazine's Man of the Year).

Everybody knows that Guatemala is a surreal country.

Those are the opening words of a letter from my grandfather, published in *Prensa Libre*, one of the country's leading newspapers, on June 8, 1954, three weeks before the overthrow of Arbenz.

Then, in a voice that is not his own, a voice that's erudite, somewhere between mythological and equivocal, my grandfather starts talking about the pact between Hun-Toh and Kabilajuj-Tsi, heads of the pre-Columbian aboriginal kingdoms, concerning, he writes, equitable distribution of the forests of Utatlán; and about the seventh stanza of the *Rabinal Achí*, in which the baron attributes the

misfortunes of his followers to the housing prob-
lem in Iximche; and about the decree by Herod
Antipas, king of the Tiberians, he writes, whose
solution to the revolt of the Essenes was to distrib-
ute teachings among the different Jewish factions;
and about the Zend-Avesta, a collection of Persian
wisdom developed by Zoroaster, whose justice, he
writes, was based on the very sound principle of
to each his due; and about some forgotten papyri
from the Book of the Dead, on which the ancient
Egyptians bequeathed us magical formulas about
the occupancy of celestial houses, he writes, by
wandering spirits.

In his overblown letter, my grandfather was
responding—probably through some lawyer or aca-
demic he had hired for the purpose—to a report
published the previous day in the same paper,
about a petition brought to President Arbenz's government by a man named Julio Ramírez Arteaga.
In his petition, Señor Ramírez Arteaga was calling
on the Guatemalan Congress to expropriate the El
Prado building, in the center of the city, of which
my grandfather was the owner.

Ramírez Arteaga, a Bolivian musician and composer of rondas, cuecas, huaynos, and other Andean

music, was traveling to a number of Latin American countries to help establish a writers' and composers' union in each one—Argentina, Uruguay, Nicaragua. And on reaching Guatemala, he had set himself up in one of the apartments in the El Prado building. Illegally, according to my grandfather's letter, signing no contract and paying no rent. Ramírez Arteaga argued in his petition to the Arbenz government that my grandfather's building ought to be inhabited only by Guatemalan artists, given that (and I quote) its comfortable apartments offer views of the beautiful volcanoes and the dazzling sunrise, which would inspire them in creating their art. But it got no further than that. Three weeks after the Bolivian musicians' petition and my grandfather's rather cynical epistolary response, Arbenz was overthrown, and Ramírez Arteaga fled Guatemala, and the expropriations stopped.

I ONLY EVER WROTE ONE LETTER to my grandfather.

It was the summer of 1981. I was about to turn ten. My parents had traveled to the United States to prepare things so we could leave

Guatemala—find someplace to live, buy furniture, enroll us in school—and in the meantime they'd left us at my grandfather's house, which was not a house, nor a palace, but, in fact, an alcázar: magnificent, ostentatious, enveloped in an air of eucalyptus and grandeur. Gala dinners were held there, with servants and butlers. Musicians, celebrities, ambassadors, even presidents would stay as guests. There's a photo of Juan Legido from Los Churumbeles de España, also known as El Gitano Señorón, singing in the living room. There's a photo of José Azzari, national celebrity and international wrestling champion, better known as El Tigre de Chiantla (and brother of the cattle rancher Azzari, whose famous herd of cows I had encountered at his farm at San Juan Acul), drinking champagne with my grandfather in the lobby, both of them in suit and bow tie. There's a photo of Golda Meir, prime minister of Israel, smiling in front of a black screen with gold dragons (years later, while lying faceup in a private room at Tokyo University, on my first trip to Japan, I would remember that one of my grandfather's fetishes had been collecting Oriental works of art: screens, engravings, ink drawings, textiles,

ceramic pots, an antique tatami with green silk
brocade that he hung on his study wall, as though
it were not a rug, but a work of art).

My grandfather, throughout dinner, had been
yelling at me about something, about anything.
That afternoon, he'd found my brother and me in a
former bathroom next to the pool, a space that was
now a small storeroom, snooping through a box-
ful of photos (running out of there, I had dropped
an old photo of his firstborn son, Salomón, as a
boy in the snow in New York in 1940). We were
used to my grandfather's yelling, to his loud and
aggressive tone, but that night, with me, he got
much worse. Maybe his rage had nothing to do
with me (or with that black-and-white photo of
the boy Salomón, whose name nobody in the family dared speak). Maybe there was something else
bothering him, or he was in a bad mood, or he'd
had a hard day. But that level of understanding is
beyond a boy who feels himself the target of a vol-
ley of shouts and insults. So great was my grandfather's fury that for a few moments he couldn't
access the words in Spanish and started yelling at
me in Arabic. Until I couldn't take it anymore. In
the middle of the dinner, I shoved my chair back

and ran up the stairs, and once in my room, crying, I sat down to write my grandfather a letter.

In all capitals, I wrote to him that I was leaving. That I didn't want to live with him anymore. That the next day I would leave his house (without the faintest idea where I intended to go). But bit by bit, as I wrote, my rage diminished, my crying abated, and I fell asleep right there, my head on the desk, on the paper.

When I woke the following morning, now in my bed (I don't remember moving there), I discovered the letter I had written my grandfather on the nightstand. I didn't know who'd put it there, whether it was my grandfather or my grandmother or maybe one of the servants, or whether anyone had read it. But there it was, in a red-and-blue post office envelope, ready for sending. And there I left it. Still in my pajamas, hungry, and smelling the pita bread that had just come out of the oven for breakfast, I left my room and was making my way down the stairs when suddenly I heard my grandfather's gruff voice from below.

You, come here.

He sounded serious, more than annoyed. I readied myself for his yelling.

I found my grandfather sitting at the backgammon table, which was already open and had the pieces set up for the start of a game.

Sit, he said, gesturing at the other stool, opposite him.

I kept quiet, a little confused. The beautiful table used for backgammon—or shesh-besh, as my grandfather called it, the Arabic for five-six—was sacred, untouchable, forbidden to us children. It was made of wood and mother-of-pearl. My grandfather had brought it from Damascus in the thirties.

Sit down, my grandfather commanded again, and so I sat on the stool opposite him, slowly, carefully, and we began to play. Or rather, my grandfather began to teach me to play. To throw the dice properly. To shout shesh-besh when the dice showed a five and a six. To carry out an instant calculation of probabilities and risks. To not touch the pieces until you were sure where to put them. To never count out loud. It was quite clear, even to a boy of nearly ten, that he was making an effort to control his impatience. And he did control it. We soon ended the game—the first of many that week, played each time I woke up and came downstairs—and then my grandfather just stood up and left the house without a word, without even saying goodbye.

WHEN SHE RETURNED FROM the Miss Universe pageant in California, Rogelia Cruz started studying architecture at the Universidad de San Carlos, and she also started collaborating more and more with the revolutionary movement. She distributed pamphlets. She took part in strikes and student demonstrations. She trained the new comrades. She transported and hid any comrades who were being pursued by the army. In 1965, the police raided her property—the family farm where she was living—and discovered weapons and chlorate containers and other bomb-making material; she was locked up for two and a half months in the Santa Teresa women's prison (and managed to get out, partly thanks to the political influence of her aunt's husband, the government's secretary of information, Baltasar Morales de la Cruz). In January 1968—exactly one year after my grandfather's kidnapping—having been captured by a paramilitary squad, her naked body turned up under the Cula-jaté bridge, close to Escuintla, along with those of eleven campesinos who had been tortured and then murdered. Her arms and legs were covered in cig-arette burns. Her wrists and ankles were bloodied by the shackles. They had bitten off her nipples and mutilated her breasts and genitals. The pathologist found poison in her stomach and signs of her hav-ing been raped repeatedly. She had died, at last, from one final blow to the skull. She was three months pregnant.

I POURED THE LAST OF THE DARK BEER into my small glass and took a warm, frothy sip while recall-ing the first time I'd been in that bar on the cor-ner of the round building, one night in the late nineties, in the company of an old painter who drank only Stolichnaya with ice and who talked a lot and possibly exaggerated a lot. There were three important things the painter told me that night, or three things that have withstood the weight of time. One: that he had grown up poor, so poor that his father—a traveling coal salesman—didn't even have the money to buy him paper and pencils, and thus he had learned to draw with his index finger in the sand his mother would scatter and smooth for him each morning on their front patio. Impermanence, he'd shouted in the bar, his index finger now drawing in the air. Mothers, he'd shouted, his eyes aflame and a little glassy. Two: that right there, he said, on one of the barstools, the musician and composer Lee Hazlewood had gotten drunk. Years back. Though my friend the painter didn't know whether it was before or after writing his most famous song, These Boots Are Made for Walkin'. Before, surely, he whispered, or that's what he'd like to think, it seemed logical to him, that right there, getting drunk on one of the stools in the old bar in Guatemala, Lee Hazlewood had come up with the idea for the song—later made famous by Nancy Sinatra—about walking all over somebody, stomping on somebody with a pair of boots. And three (drinking his fifth or sixth Stolichnaya with ice): that that woman was ours. Those were his words: That woman is ours, his voice weary, referring to the huge black mural he'd painted as a tribute, on a building at the Universidad de San Carlos, in 1973, of the face of Rogelia Cruz.

OR HAD MY GRANDFATHER SEEN, there in El Espinero, the safe house where they were holding him, not a beauty queen among all the other guerrillas coming and going in the darkness, but the lady with the marimbas and the red coat?

WE COULD HEAR THE MARIMBAS from some distance. My father had parked the jade green Volvo station wagon on Séptima Avenida, and despite his instructions that we were all to go in together, that we were to wait for him and my mother and sister, my brother and I walked quickly toward the huge converted depot with the wooden columns and red tiled roof, toward the smell of sweet smoke and sizzling meat, toward the music of the marimbas. My father roared at us again, an almost mythic bellow, as the two of us walked as fast as we could past a beggar crawling on hands and knees along the sidewalk.

El Rodeo. That's what the restaurant was called. One of the few family restaurants in Guatemala in the seventies, and perhaps the only one in the city open for lunch on Sundays. I remember it always full, and everything inside being big, or at least looking big from my child's perspective: the thick mahogany tables, the chairs upholstered in black-and-white cowhide, the heavy leather menus, the bull's head on the front wall just inside the door, the long grill where half a dozen overheated men were cooking. In fact, all the people who worked at that restaurant were men—cooks, waiters, bartend-ers, musicians—and all of them wore the same uni-form: black pants, white long-sleeved shirt, black bow tie.

Did you not hear me?, shouted my father, furious.

My brother and I were still at the entrance, try-ing to see the two marimbas in the back corner.

We have to go in together, yelled my father. Not like animals.

Let's go, kids, said my mother, carrying my three-year-old sister and steering us toward a table, which was, to our misfortune, too far from the marimbas.

It was the same ritual every Sunday. We would walk to the table with our mother while our father greeted friends and acquaintances at the other tables; we would sit down, taking care to leave him the seat with the best view of the front door (I want to see who's coming in, he would declare); my brother and I would order and immediately consume our one soft drink of the day; and then we would sit, quiet and well behaved, until our father finally showed up, all smiles, always with the same question:

Do you know what you want to eat?

My father called over the waiter and placed orders for tenderloin and rib eye, guacamole, grilled scallions, a basket of garlic bread. The waiter took away the two empty bottles. Under the table, my brother kicked me.

Now?, I asked. My father frowned, shaking his head. Ten minutes, he said with some distaste, and my brother and I smiled and pushed back our enormous black-and-white chairs and ran off toward the marimbas.

We didn't like the marimba music. Or not especially. What we liked was to watch the marimba players, watch their mallets in motion, watch the almost perfect coordination of the sticks of guava wood and rubber in the hands of those dark-skinned, uniformed, expressionless men.

There were four men that Sunday: two per marimba. One of them might have been blind or partially blind (his eyes had a milky look), but he moved his mallets just like the other three. We stood in front of them, watching in silence, fascinated in silence, until the piece of music ended and the half-blind guy put one of the sticks in his mouth and started biting the little rubber ball, and at the same time we heard our father behind us, calling. Those ten minutes were never enough.

Sit down, boys, said my mother, the meat's getting cold.

The grilled sirloin, buttered baked potatoes, and roasted corn were steaming on my plate. I was already old enough to use a steak knife. Proudly, carefully, I began to cut my meat.

That lady, over there, the one in the red coat, whispered my father, but I didn't know if this was directed at me or at my mother or at the whole table. And then, gesturing toward the front door with his chin, he whispered again: She was one of the guerrillas who kidnapped my father.

The marimbas started.

I was nearly nine at the time and knew very little about my grandfather's kidnapping. But I'd always imagined his kidnappers the way you would, as a child, imagine all villains: smelly, fat, hairy, missing two or three teeth, with oily faces covered in warts and pimples and scars. I had never imagined a lady. Let alone a beautiful lady, all dressed up, proud and preening in her red coat.

Want some garlic bread?, asked my father, offering us the basket.

I reached out a hand and grabbed a piece of hard, greasy bread. But I miscalculated and took too big a bite. I chewed with difficulty, my mouth half-open, as the lady in the red coat greeted people and laughed with people and seemed to float over to her table right beside the marimbas.

No, THAT'S NOT HOW IT HAPPENED. Or that's what my father told me one chilly, wet afternoon when he was visiting me in Paris.

We were walking down Boulevard Raspail to the small office I'd been assigned on Columbia University's Paris campus as part of a fellowship to live and work there for a year. Suddenly we found ourselves passing Captain Dreyfus (sculpted and erected in the Place Pierre-Lafue by the Polish artist Louis Mitelberg, also known as Tim), and I don't know why, perhaps owing to the image and the symbolism of the captain's broken sword, I started to tell my father my recollections of that Sunday. And my father just listened patiently, in silence, until we came to the noisy intersection of Boulevard Raspail and Boulevard du Montparnasse. But it wasn't a Sunday, he insisted, frowning, his voice too loud, maybe because of the noise from the traffic or maybe to emphasize his opinion. And that the lady wasn't wearing a red coat. And that it wasn't in El Rodeo, either, but in a seafood restaurant in an old warehouse in Zona 9, called Delicias del Mar, the owner of which was the brother of my uncle by marriage. I didn't want to get into an argument with my father in the middle of Paris, in front of a somber and majestic Balzac (whom Rodin had, in turn, encased in a coat of bronze), and I just kept quiet and we went on walking through the now almost dark city.

My father's memory used to be remarkable, particularly for rumor and gossip, but I think when it came to this recollection he was mistaken. Impossible, unacceptable, that the scene with the guerrilla woman all decked out in red could have happened in a seafood restaurant owned by a Jew.

AND RIGHT ON TIME, WITHOUT HER RED COAT, she finally came in through the door of the bar on the corner of the round building.

THOUGH IT HAD BEEN MORE THAN thirty years since that Sunday at a steak house, or possibly a seafood restaurant, I recognized her at once. Her long hair was no longer tar black, but a dazzling, almost iridescent silver (a faint white bulb swayed from the ceiling, immediately above her, and I thought of the scales of a fish moving in and out of a beam of light). The skin on her face looked more tanned than naturally brown. I didn't remember her being that tall and thin. Nor did I remember the honey color of her eyes or the tiny black mole that looked drawn on, beside her mouth. She was wearing blue gabardine pants, battered old cowboy boots, and a light blouse in white cotton with an embroidered pattern typical of the Guatemalan highlands. From her neck, above her cleavage, hung a jade cross.

I stumbled slightly in my desire to stand up, a bit nervous at her presence or at her beauty or at the question that struck me when I saw her floating once again toward me: if a person who has once committed murder, whatever their motive for killing, is forever a murderer, what is a person who once kidnapped and tortured?

YOU'RE HALFON, SHE SAID, holding out a delicate hand. Unmistakable, she added, though I couldn't understand why. She exchanged a fleeting glance with the notary, who had just limped back out of the bathroom—without his cigarette or his glass of whiskey—or maybe she didn't and I just thought I'd seen them exchanging a fleeting glance, more hostile than complicit. I said I was pleased to meet her, and thanked her for accepting my invitation. Before letting go of her hand, or before allowing her to let go of mine, I had made an instant calculation to determine how many years there were between us. And I was still calculating, rounding the number down, when I heard the rustle of the bartender dragging his feet, heading toward us. She greeted him like a lifelong friend (How's it going, Pancho?) and asked him for another Negra Modelo for me and one for her. And a couple of tequilas, too, right?, she added, staring at me or challenging me. I smiled the rancid smile of a vanquished man as I watched her gather all my things off the table and put them mysteriously on the table next to us. Pointless to ask why. Well, she said, now seated at the other table and pulling out a Camel from my pack without asking. I don't know how I can help you, but here I am.

No sooner had I entered the enormous hall of the Guatemala Book Fair, in midmorning, lost amid the attendees and the book stalls and still trying to locate the events room—where I was due to give the opening speech in just a few minutes—than I was approached by a gentleman in a long white gown and black cap who came over to greet me and tell me in hushed, respectful tones how much he admired my work, before holding out both hands to present me with a copy of the Qu'ran. He explained, as he gave me three other books about Islam, that he was the director of the Guatemalan Muslim Association, and they would be honored if I might visit their mosque. I murmured a few words of thanks—genuine ones, since nobody had ever presented me with this sacred text before or invited me to visit their mosque—and I started to move away down the aisle. But I hadn't taken five steps before another gentleman, portlier than the first and not remotely respectful, came up immediately to reproach me, with a snide smile, for having blocked him on social media. I stammered a few words of apology—less sincere this time—and said I needed to hurry to get to the opening event, where they were waiting for me, and the gentleman, with wine or possibly vinegar on his breath, yelled at my departing back: Oh well of course, off you go then, asshole. I slipped down the aisle quickly and still needed to ask for help from a young lady in uniform, who looked like she might be an employee or a volunteer, before finding the room at the end of the hall. And I was about to go in, at last, when a potbellied old man with a tangled beard grabbed hold of my forearm and stopped me at the threshold. He had the sticky gaze of someone who has just woken up. He was wearing a dirty, wrinkled shirt. The end of his belt was hanging loose, flimsy, unbuckled. His face was familiar, and I assumed he was a Colombian journalist at whose house I'd had a bowl of ajiaco for dinner many years earlier. I said what a pleasure it was to see him again, and how delicious the ajiaco had been that night, but he would have to excuse me, because I needed to go into the hall, where they were waiting for me to start the event. He frowned. He went on gripping my forearm, his long nails piercing my skin. I see you've been doing well, Halfon, he said, not without some malice and with no trace of any Colombian accent. And then, with a hyena laugh, and finally extracting his nails from my forearm, he added: You're no longer kidnappable.

Confused, I almost ran into the room.

It wasn't until fifteen or twenty minutes later, when I was in the middle of trying to deliver a short speech I had memorized phonetically in Kaqchikel (about the importance of our getting closer, as Guatemalan Ladinos, to the world of our Mayan compatriots, since that year the book fair was dedicated to the country's more than twenty indigenous languages), that I realized that the bearded old man had been one of the guerrillas involved in planning the kidnapping of my grandfather.

El Sordo. The deaf one. I remember they used to call him that, maliciously. Because of his big ears.

I was forced to sit on the stage for almost an hour, enduring the tedious, demagogic speeches by assorted ambassadors and ministers, but the whole time thinking about his strange comment (what had he been trying to tell me?, why was I no longer kidnappable?, because of my political ideas?, because of the paltriness of my writer's bank account?), before I was able to escape and seek him out in the crowd.

I found him in the same place, standing by the entrance to the room, as if he hadn't moved from there during all the lengthy formalities, or as if he now wished to say goodbye to each of the attendees as they filed out. He was holding a glass of white wine in one hand and a small dish with chips and guacamole and black beans in the other. Want some?, he asked, holding the dish out to me.

113

I'm sure you'd like them, he said. They're Turkish canapés, and again he laughed loudly.

HER NAME WAS SARA. Or at least that was her nom de guerre, her name among the guerrillas. Sara. Or Sarita. Or Saraguate (some people said that this nickname, which was the local word for a howler monkey, was merely a natural extension of her own name or pseudonym; others, more daring or spiteful, said she'd been given the moniker by an old comrade and lover because of the way she howled in bed). She'd spent many years in exile, in Cuba, in Nicaragua, in Mexico, in France, but she was back now and living on a farm on the outskirts of San Juan Sacatepéquez. The hard part hadn't been tracking down her phone number (El Sordo, after a few glasses of white wine and a bit of persuasion, had given it to me), or locating her (she belonged to one of the best-known families of artists and intellectuals in the country); the hard part had been summoning up the courage to dial that number and introduce myself and say I wanted to talk to her. To talk about your grandfather, I suppose, her voice had interrupted me on the telephone, guessing my intentions, and I said yes, about my grandfather. Then she had remained silent for a few seconds, which felt like minutes or years. Very well, Halfon, but first I need to tell you two things. And she inhaled loud and long, as if gathering her breath before diving down into the deep and telling me those two things. First, she said, I'll meet you only because I feel like I owe it to your family. I didn't say anything, though I could have said many things. And second, she said, I'm asking you to never, under any circumstances, write anything about what we discuss. Alright?

THERE ARE SEVERAL REASONS the guerrillas decided to kidnap my grandfather in January of 1967.

The first, the official one, was that as the owner of a fabric shop (El Paje, in the Portal del Comercio), a textile factory (Lacetex, on Avenida Bolívar), and previously a coffee plantation (in El Tumbador, San Marcos), he had treated his employees badly. My own memory of my grandfather is of a proper, upright, strict boss, with employees who

were very loyal despite his domineering and sometimes irascible nature. And although in terms of
their labor he might have treated them just like
every other Guatemalan businessman treated (and
still treats) his workers—no decent wages, no ade-
quate benefits, no fair contract, no possibility of
organizing in a union—I don't believe this was the
true reason for his kidnapping.

I find the second explanation much more accept-
able, or at least feasible: money. The guerillas wanted, needed, financing. During the years of the civil
war, the guerrillas kidnapped two types of people.
One: politicians and soldiers, to get revenge for
something or to use them as pawns in negotiations
when demanding the freedom of other imprisoned
guerrilla fighters. And two: businessmen, to finance
their campaigns with ransoms and thereby, they
maintained, give the people back part of the wealth
that the businessmen had taken from them. This
explanation, money, seems much more honest to
me, albeit still inhuman, still bloodthirsty.

But there was another reason or explanation
for the kidnapping of my grandfather. A third one.
A secret one. One that nobody in the family ever
knew. One that now, after a long night of tequila

and smoke and honey-eyed looks, I alone know: my grandfather's name was given to the guerrilla forces by another Jew. By one of his friends from the synagogue. By one of his companions in Saturday prayers. By somebody who knew him very well, and who knew the value of the name he was handing over, and who probably received something in exchange. A Jew wrote another Jew's name on a slip of paper and handed that slip of paper over to his torturers. Eduardo Halfon, barely legible, in pencil.

I WAS A LONG WAY AWAY, starting college in North Carolina, when my grandfather died.

It was late autumn. My father called me at college to tell me that my grandfather had died of a heart attack (he had been in the hospital for several days but had suffered from heart trouble for years), that he was to be buried the following morning at the Jewish cemetery in Guatemala. And his voice cracked. He was breathing fast, as if short of oxygen, as if making an effort not to burst into tears, as if crying over the death of a father was forbidden. And I, owing to my physical

distance or my emotional distance, felt sadder for
him than for the death of my grandfather. But I
wasn't to travel to Guatemala, he said when he was
able to talk again, I wouldn't arrive in time for the
burial, and it was best for me to focus on my final
exams. It was my first semester studying engineering. I was on the verge of failing every one of my
courses. And my father, though he didn't know
this, perhaps sensed it. Best for me to focus on
my final exams, I heard him repeat over the telephone as I lay in my dorm bed. Then, after a short
but uncomfortable silence, he said that he and his
sisters had already begun the process of emptying
everything out (my grandfather's house or man-
sion or palace would be dismantled and knocked
down a couple of years later, the land used for
three modern office buildings), and that in one of
the study's bookcases they had found a small box
he'd left me. An old shoe box, he said, with something inside. Want me to open it?

Outside, in the hallway, I could hear students
yelling, outrageously drunk. I said to my father of
course, but to give me a minute, so I could shut the
door. That moment, I knew despite my immatu-
rity, held the glimmer of a black stone in the rain.

My father opened the box and told me that my grandfather had left me a few things: a heavy metal seal that stamped paper with his name in relief, which is also my name in relief; a pack of small sky blue business cards with his name engraved in gray letters, which is also my name engraved in gray letters; one last sheaf of fine letter-size paper with his name printed in the top left corner, which is also my name printed in the top left corner. My father was telling me something else, but I wasn't paying attention as I tried to picture that metal seal, those sky blue cards, that fine paper. My grandfather had left me these things because I was the only person who could still use them, because I was the only other Eduardo Halfon. My inheritance, literally, textually, was my name.

So do you want me to open it or don't you?, insisted my father, exasperated.

Inside the shoe box, I understood at last, was something else. An old letter on red-and-blue stationery from the post office. It was the letter that I had written my grandfather in the summer of 1981, after that dinner with all the yelling in Arabic, and which had been left forgotten on the nightstand.

SEÑOR ELÍAS WAS ALONE IN HIS OFFICE in the Elma building, facing the central plaza, wrapping up the brown paper package with string and masking tape. But suddenly he had to stop and take a swig from the bottle of aged rum he kept in the credenza behind his desk. He would never forget that this was the only time in the whole process that his hands trembled uncontrollably.

My grandfather, on the first day of the kidnapping, as soon as he arrived at the safe house and found himself without the black hood, had told the guerrillas that they should immediately contact Señor Elías—his accountant, his old Lebanese friend, his companion every Thursday at the Turkish baths at the Industrial Club—to act as intermediary. Señor Elías, my grandfather had told them, was the most loyal and most honest person he knew (unlike—as the decades that followed would show—President Jorge Serrano Elías, his nephew, who fled the country with millions of stolen dollars in 1993, having suspended the constitution and dissolved Congress and the Supreme Court and failed in his attempt to install himself in power in perpetuity; and also unlike Vice President Roxana Baldetti Elías, his granddaughter, sentenced to fifteen years in prison in 2017 for embezzlement and fraud).

Señor Elías spent more than a month meeting with the kidnappers. Always in person. And always in different locations around the city. First he would receive a call, there, at his office in the Elma building, and the same voice would inform him of an inexact date and time and place. In Fu Lu Sho restaurant, at night. In the bar at the Ritz Hotel, midmorning. In Morazán Park, midafternoon. In Pasaje Aycinena, midnight. On the left-hand bench facing the presidential palace, before dawn. Señor Elías, then, was to show up and wait. Finally two or three men would appear. They would say only a number and Señor Elías would tell them he'd consult with the family of the kidnapped man and give them an answer at the next meeting. Nothing by telephone. Nothing in writing. No names. No looking each other in the eye. But years later, when he arrived at his office one morning and opened the newspaper and saw a notice from the government offering a ten-thousand-quetzal reward for information leading to a capture, Señor Elías would recognize the taciturn, childlike face of the one kid-napper who came to every meeting. Canción.

MERY RAMÍREZ WAS STANDING on the corner of Sexta Avenida and Décima Calle. She was wearing a black dress, black hat, black tights, and black heels, as she'd been instructed, and she was sweat-ing in the midday sun. She was a dark woman, plump, not tall; seen from above, she might have looked like a black dot amid the grayish torrent of pedestrians in the city center. In her hands she held a thick brown paper package (already covered in smudges from her damp hands), tied up tight with string and sealed with masking tape. She had been waiting over an hour. That was all they had told her. That she was to wait at noon on the cor-ner of Sexta Avenida and Décima Calle, dressed entirely in black, with the brown paper package in her hands, because that was what my grandfa-ther had asked of her. She, his lifelong secretary, according to my grandfather's instructions, was the only person he trusted to carry out the han-dover. Mery Ramírez felt the passersby shoving her, brushing past her, bumping the package in her hands. And she felt her legs starting to give way, trembling slightly, out of tiredness or nerves. Her vision turned blurry and she almost didn't see when a man went by and snatched the parcel from her and disappeared into the throng. She remained there a moment, motionless. She didn't know what to do. She didn't know if she ought to chase after him. She wasn't sure if he had been the assigned man or just some thief. And right there, as if she were being swallowed up by the sea of pedestrians in the city center, Mery Ramírez dropped to her knees and began to pray.

FOUR GUERRILLAS WOKE MY GRANDFATHER very early. They said nothing. They just kicked his cot repeatedly until he stood up. Then they stuck the barrel of a gun in his side and led him out.

Dawn was only just breaking. But my grandfather—as his eyes adjusted to the dim light—managed to notice two things. First: on the street, waiting for them with the engine running and the four doors open, was an old Dodge Dart (El

Tortugón, the guerrillas called it, but no one now could remember whether this was because of its moss green color, or because it moved as slowly as a turtle, or both). And second: just before they once again covered his face with a black hood and put him in the backseat, my grandfather looked up and saw the silhouette of a man atop the roof of the house where they'd been holding him; he held a shotgun in his left hand, while with his right he was unscrewing a red lightbulb.

They drove slowly and in silence through the city for hours—or that's how it felt to my grandfather, guarded by a guerrilla on either side—as if they were going around in circles to throw off anybody who might be following them. Until at last they stopped.

The engine was still running. Nobody inside moved. No one spoke. My grandfather could still feel the barrel of the gun in his side. Suddenly he heard one of the guerrillas open a door. Another of the guerrillas took off my grandfather's black hood. Another shoved him out and my grandfather fell facedown onto a vacant lot of dry dirt. And sprawled there, on that vacant lot under the Trébol bridge, my grandfather watched the Dodge

Dart drive off, in no hurry. A moss green silhouette amid the traffic and hubbub of Avenida Roosevelt.

He waited a few minutes longer, just lying there on the ground, but he couldn't remember why. Maybe simply catching his breath. Maybe scared the Dodge Dart might turn around and the guerrillas would come back for him. Maybe trying to rid himself of the sensation that overcame him, a sensation of total invisibility: all the passersby (he would not forget this) would walk right past him and almost over him without looking, without even batting an eye.

Slowly, cautiously, he got to his feet, shook the dust off his pants, and began to walk—though I always imagined him flying—the four and a half kilometers to the big front gate of his house on Avenida Reforma.

AFTER THIRTY-FIVE DAYS OF CAPTIVITY, a substantial ransom had been paid (I wonder what happened to that brown paper package, what it might have bought, who ended up with all the dollars inside it). My grandfather was in good health, under the

circumstances. He said that, under the circumstances, his captors had treated him with decency.
In his trouser pocket, he still had the wad of quetzals for the construction workers, untouched. On
his left pinkie finger, he still wore his ring with
the three-carat diamond. His two gold pens he'd
given to one of the kidnappers: the politest (Señor
Halfon, the man had called him, according to my
grandfather); the one who shared unsmokable cigarettes with him, dark-tobacco cigarettes called
Payasos (six cents a pack, according to my grandfather); the one who each morning brought him a
rusty military canteen full of coffee (insipid instant
coffee, my grandfather said); the one who each
night asked what he wanted for dinner (an anchovy
pizza from Vesuvio, according to my grandfather);
the one who played a round of dominoes with
him every evening (he always let the man win, my
grandfather said, to keep him happy); the one who
had chronic migraines (according to my grandfather, he himself had on several occasions sent someone out to the pharmacy for salts and medicine);
the one who had, bit by bit, negotiated the cost of
the ransom with him (my grandfather got annoyed
when he learned the total paid by his family, since

he'd managed to negotiate a much lower sum with this guerrilla). He couldn't remember his name, or perhaps he never knew it.

My grandfather used to say that, in the first days of the kidnapping, he had his bankbook in his trouser pocket, and he sensed that he ought to get rid of it as soon as possible, so as not to give the kidnappers any financial information. He said he'd thought about waiting until they took him to the bathroom and throwing it into the toilet, but that he was worried he'd clog up the plumbing. He said that he then thought of tearing it into pieces and throwing it in the trash—or out the window, he sometimes said—but he was afraid the kidnappers would find it and put it back together. He had no other option, said my grandfather, but to eat it.

THIRTY-FIVE NIGHTS HE HAD SLEPT in the same old cot of rotten wood and green canvas that smelled of sweat and urine. A green canvas that— my grandfather was well aware—the army had forbidden the city's textile dealers from selling. The old cot had been stolen by the guerrillas from a military barracks in Poptún, after they'd been victorious in a battle deep inside the Petén jungle (PROPERTY OF THE GUATEMALAN ARMY was stenciled in black on the reverse of the green canvas). Every morning, when he woke up, my grandfather said he would shake it, fold it up, and lean it against the wall of the small room where he was being held. Take good care of that old rot, his captors would say to him, laughing at their own joke.

THIRTY-FIVE NIGHTS HE'D FALLEN ASLEEP to the sound of a guitar. In the distance, in some other room of the safe house, one of the guerrillas played his guitar at night. My grandfather never knew who. Perhaps a lookout.

THIRTY-FIVE NIGHTS HE'D DREAMED the same dream. My grandfather would recount it years later, when he was nearing the end of his life, to the old man with the sky blue eyes and Bedouin face who had once been able to read the future in damp coffee grounds (maybe Uncle Salomón's being half sorcerer was why my grandfather had decided to confide his dream to him); and then that old Bedouin, at the end of his life, told it to me. Each night of the kidnapping, said my grandfather, he dreamed of a fish swimming in a lagoon or a lake. It was not a beautiful fish. Nor especially violent. Nor especially large. Nor did it speak. It was just a fish that appeared in his dreams every night—undoubtedly a hyperbole—swimming just beneath the surface of a lagoon or a lake. But after the kidnapping, after those thirty-five nights, my grandfather told him, he never dreamed of the fish again. As if the fish had lived and swum not in a lagoon or a lake, but right there, in the safe house where my grandfather was being held. Or as if, after the kidnapping, the fish no longer had any meaning in my grandfather's conscious life, nor in my grandfather's subconscious life, and had chosen to remain there, in the past, kind of floating in the darkness of those thirty-five nights. The old Bedouin then asked my grandfather how he interpreted that recurring dream about a fish, if he believed that the recurring dream about a fish might have some deeper or more obscure meaning.

And my grandfather, who was always categorical, the old Bedouin told me, just gave a quick wave of his hand, as if wiping such an absurd question out of the air.

CLINT EASTWOOD IS HOLDING a dark-tobacco cigarette loosely between his lips. He's got a brown poncho over his shoulders and an elegant yet scruffy leather hat. From his serious, dusty expression, he looks like he's about to shoot. Though we cannot see the revolver. The magazine photo is cut in half, just under his neck. But staring at it closely, I could imagine the old revolver perfectly, and his finger already on the trigger, ready to fire. I held out a hand and placed it on the photo of Clint Eastwood, still a young man, smoking in the desert in one of his many Westerns—Sergio Leone's *A Fistful of Dollars?*—and I pushed the swinging door as if I were pushing the swinging door of a cowboy saloon.

The bathroom was smaller than I remembered, dirtier and darker. There was no soap or toilet paper. There was no toilet seat or cover. No water came out of the tap. A single white bulb flickered in a poorly installed ceiling light; from time to time it would go out for a second or two, and it seemed like it would never come back on again. But it always did. Maybe it was the poor lighting, or maybe it was having had so many tequilas, but my face in the mirror looked like the face of somebody much older. I smiled at the old man in the mirror. It's possible he did not smile back.

I approached the toilet without actually touching it, and shut my eyes. I felt euphoric, somewhere between lustful and drunk, as if bloated with so many images and so much information. I felt slightly dizzy and staggered a little (I've never been able to drink) and I could make out, in the distance, the white buzz of a bar closing at the end of the night: glasses and chairs and inconsequential muted voices that no one is listening to anymore. When I opened my eyes again, I could see, in the gloom, that there were two words written on the wall in front of me. Two words in black ink. Two words in capitals. Two words that had probably been there for many years, or maybe not.

Be careful.

CANCIÓN'S BODY WASHED UP on the bank of the Suchiate River.

He had been hiding out in Mexico City for some time. His name was not Percy now, or Ramiro, but Abraham (Abraham López Ramírez). And there, right in the center of the city, along with another Guatemalan guerrilla who was likewise in exile (Ricardo Arévalo Bocaletti), he had opened a modest butcher shop. Once again, Canción had disguised himself as a butcher. Once again, Canción sold cuts of meat and sausages to the ladies in the neighborhood. Until he showed up dead in the Suchiate River.

No one ever knew for certain who killed him. Some speculated that it had been the Mexican police—because at the end of 1971, they identified Abraham as Canción and arrested him in his small shop while he was working as a butcher, knife in hand, still wearing his white apron stained red. Some speculated that it had been the Germans—because of his personal involvement in the kidnapping and murder of the German ambassador to Guatemala, Karl von Spreti. Some speculated that it had been the CIA—because of his personal involvement in the murder of the U.S. ambassador to Guatemala, John Gordon Mein. Some speculated that it had been one of his enemies in the Rebel Armed Forces—because Canción was one of the guerrillas accused by his comrades, privately and publicly, of betrayal and embezzlement of funds and of keeping ransom money, of pocketing it for himself (he needed that money to survive, he replied). And some speculated, of course, that it had been the Guatemalan military or the Guatemalan government or the oligarchic Guatemalan family of one of his victims—for revenge.

Some campesinos found his body floating by the bank of the river that marks the border between Guatemala and Mexico. He had taken a single bullet to the forehead. I like to imagine that the moment he died, when he took that single bullet to the forehead, he had the two gold pens that my grandfather had given him in his pocket, and that he'd tried trading them for his life. Sometimes I imagine him on his knees and blindfolded and begging on the muddy banks of the Suchiate River. Other times, I imagine him up to his waist in the

Suchiate River, hands behind his back, telling the person holding the gun to please look in his pocket, that he's got a couple of really valuable gold pens, a couple of gold pens that are his most prized war trophies. And others still, I imagine Canción suddenly turning into a singer in the Suchiate River and singing his killer a song that is both sad and sweet, about a Lebanese Jew who long ago gave a guerrilla fighter a couple of dazzling gold pens, one final song before the crack of one final bullet exploding in the dark tropical night.

Kimono on the Skin

Her name was Aiko. She had short black hair, big black eyes, skin like glass. I didn't recognize her until she, blushing, agreed to put on the same white mask she had been wearing the night before at the Tokyo airport.

I really liked what you just said in your talk, she said in correct English as she took her mask back off. About being the grandson of a Lebanese man who isn't Lebanese, she added. Shakrun, I said. Shukran, you mean, she said, correcting me, and I adjusted my disguise a bit, and she maybe sensed my evasion, because immediately she launched into some explanation about Lebanese identity. No more than thirty, I thought. No more than twenty, I thought. No idea, I thought, resigned by that point. Everything about her was a contradiction. For instance: she wore a short plaid skirt, schoolgirl-style, but at the same time had antique reading glasses hanging from her neck, like a grandmother. For instance: the skin on her face was taut and rosy as a teenager's, but at the same time one silvery gray strand sparkled in her hair, almost lost in the black expanse. For instance: the toenails of her almost bare feet were painted cherry red, but at the same time she wore a university name tag pinned to her white blouse. She'd said to me, when she introduced herself, that she was with the university. Said it like that: with. And I wasn't sure if that meant she worked at the university or was studying at the university or what.

We were standing in the auditorium where the conference was taking place, surrounded by the audience and the other participants, all of whom were also standing around us, chatting in hushed tones, paper cups of coffee in their hands. It was midmorning. Fifteen-minute break, we'd been told.

You see, I know a bit about the Lebanese diaspora, Aiko said. I'm married to a Lebanese man. And she held up her left hand to show me the proof on her ring finger, or perhaps to scare me off. Me too, I said, holding up my left hand in turn, despite no sign of any ring, and feeling like an idiot. Although not to a Lebanese man, I added, and Aiko almost smiled. You never talked about any of this with your grandfather?, she asked. No, never, I said, taking a sip of coffee. My grandfather died in my first year of university, I said, and I was never mature enough or curious enough to talk to him about growing up in Beirut, about the journey he made with his siblings, about his stay in Paris, about his eventual arrival in Guatemala. Too bad, she said. Yes, too bad. We were silent a few seconds. So are you from Tokyo?, I asked, and she said she was only there because of the university, that her family was originally from Hiroshima. I'm going early tomorrow, I told her. To Hiroshima?, she asked in surprise (she pronounced the word Hiroshima as if inhaling it). Of course. You have a commitment at the university, I imagine? No, no commitment, I said, I just want to see the city. Her brow was still furrowed. So do you still have family in Hiroshima? Aiko was silent for a moment, as though weighing up her response. My grandfather, she said, and then hastened to answer the question

137

I didn't dare ask: Yes, he's a survivor of the bomb. But she didn't say anything else and I didn't want to ask anything else and simply stood watching her nibble the edge of her paper cup.

AFTER THE BREAK, I WAS ONCE AGAIN handed the mic to read a few pages from my books to the audience. I had planned to read (in English, with simultaneous interpretation into Japanese) four excerpts from four different books recounting aspects of my grandfather's life, but I succeeded in reading only the first, about a coffee farm he'd had in the fifties or sixties, in El Tumbador, near the border with Mexico, which he sold at the start of the civil war between the military and the guerillas—a farm I had never seen. After I finished reading, I don't know why, perhaps because I didn't want to read or speak about my grandfather anymore, or perhaps because the image of that farm (or that civil war) ricocheted and activated the image of another farm, I began telling them the story of an old Guatemalan by the name of Azzari.

He was the son of an Italian who'd arrived

in Guatemala at roughly the same time as my grandfather, I said (the simultaneous interpreter, though slightly thrown by my ricochet, pressed on valiantly with his work). I met him at his cattle farm in San Juan Acul, a village in the Cuchumatanes Mountains, where for years he'd been producing cheese using a recipe that Azzari senior had brought from his small Piedmont town, Re, situated a few kilometers from the Swiss-Italian border. An artisanal, exquisite cheese, though its real secret was not the recipe, Azzari told me, but the loving care he gave his cows.

He told me that in the seventies and eighties there had been a major military base nearby (that whole part of the country, known as the Ixil region, was among those most devastated by the civil war), and somehow the soldiers at the base had found out he was giving clandestine aid to the indigenous community of San Juan Acul. Azzari never told me what type of aid he'd given the indigenous people, but I imagined it was much more than work and food. He told me that several members of the community had visited him one afternoon to warn him that the military were coming to look for him. A figure of speech, he said, meaning something far worse. Be careful, they told him. So that very night, Azzari fled the farm with his entire herd. He didn't explain how he managed to transport so many cows, whether on foot or on horseback or maybe in several trucks or wagons, but I like to picture him standing in the Cuchumatanes Mountains with a herd of huge black-and-white cows—guiding them, prodding them, stroking them, whispering words of encouragement to them so as to shepherd them from danger (several cows, no doubt descendants of that cardinal herd, were now grazing and lurking in the meadow before us). The day after his escape, at six in the morning, Azzari told me, as he and his cows were wandering through the mountains, more than a hundred soldiers entered San Juan Acul with an indigenous man, his head covered by a black ski mask. Despite the mask hiding his face, the whole town recognized him immediately. He was one of my son's friends, Azzari told me. They played together as boys. The soldiers had threatened to kill him if he didn't tell them which of the townspeople were collaborating with the guerrillas. And so all the men of San Juan Acul were paraded one by one past their black-masked companion, as he stood like an executioner in the town square, in front of the church. This one to heaven, the masked man would say, and the man was saved. This one to hell, the masked man would say, and the soldiers moved that man off to one side. In the end, eighteen men were singled out and moved toward hell; eighteen men were covered with earth and branches and dried leaves; eighteen men, following the military commander's orders, were trampled by the other men of San Juan Acul—that is, by their own friends and brothers. Then the soldiers put the eighteen bruised and naked men in front of a common grave and, with the rest of the town watching, with friends and family as their audience, began to murder them. A single bullet to the head. One by one. The eighteen men fell into that black hole in the ground until it was full of arms and legs and men. But several were still alive, only just, howling, so one of the soldiers jumped down and plunged his machete into their necks. The massacre was finished. It wasn't even noon. Azzari fell silent and let the silence spread between us like a dirty rag. Then he told me that, days or weeks after his escape, he had finally made it with his herd of cows to a friend's farm on the outskirts of the capital. It had been a long and complicated journey. And once there, once safe, they informed him that, the day after his escape, the same soldiers had indeed come looking for him on his farm in San Juan Acul, and they'd burned it down.

Aiko was waiting for me at the door to the auditorium, and we walked together to the university restaurant, we sat together at the long crowded table, we ignored—throughout the entire ramen luncheon—the other Lebanese writers and Japanese academics, we spoke in whispers about our lives and our partners (hers lived far away, she told me, in Beirut; mine, I told her, lived everywhere) while under the table I felt or thought I felt or would have liked to have felt, secretly, discreetly, our thighs repeatedly brushing.

My grandfather's kimono remained on his skin.

The café was located a couple of blocks from the university, in an old wooden house that looked like it was about to be swallowed up by all the buildings and all the modernity around it. But it's resisting, Aiko had said to me when we walked in. We were sitting on metal stools covered in maroon vinyl at a long cold gray marble counter stained with coffee and tobacco and who knows what else. On the other side of the counter, a man with disheveled white hair prepared our coffee using a strange contraption, a kind of cylindrical siphon that dripped down into a smaller round siphon and looked like something out of a chemistry lab. The disheveled man, with his white apron and white gloves, was the mad scientist.

Aiko had told me, after lunch, that this was where she most liked to have coffee, that it was her favorite place when she wanted to be alone, that we had a little time before the afternoon panels started up.

Only once did I see the burns on my grandfather's back, she said.

The cup of coffee steamed in her hands. Her tiny cherry toes didn't even reach the floor.

One morning, she said, when I was a girl, he took me swimming under a bridge on the river Ota, near his house. We were alone, holding hands. When we got there, my grandfather sat me on the

143

riverbank and walked to the water and took his robe off in front of me, with his back to me. I was young, I understood very little, but I can remember perfectly the pattern of the burn on his back. It was as though his kimono had been imprinted onto his skin, or as if someone had drawn the cloth of his kimono onto his skin. Something like that. I didn't understand why my grandfather was wearing his kimono directly on his skin. All I understood was that that those scars on his back were just like the fabric of his kimonos, kimonos I knew so well. But I didn't say anything, or ask anything. And I wasn't afraid. I just got undressed and swam in the river with my grandfather. That night, I asked my mother and she explained a little, not much, I suppose so I wouldn't be frightened. White fabric, my mother told me, repelled the bomb's heat. Dark fabric absorbed it and conducted it to the skin. My grandfather's kimono was black.

An old man walked into the café and sat down beside Aiko, greeting her as if they knew each other, and I got the sense that the old man came every day and sat on the same stool, at the same time of the afternoon.

I was just a girl, Aiko whispered, her bare knee

at times lightly grazing mine (or was I imagining it?). But that night I understood my grandfather. I understood the reason for his silence. I understood that the bomb had forever marked his skin not with just any old article of clothing, not with a shirt or jacket, but with one of the traditional kimonos he had inherited from his father and his grandfather, and which no longer even existed. The bomb had incinerated it, Aiko said. Or, rather, the bomb had embedded it in his skin.

The disheveled man approached us, the siphon of coffee in his hand; without asking, he refilled our cups. The old man next to Aiko had his head turned toward me and was staring straight at me.

Hibakusha, Aiko said. It means bombarded person, she said. That's what they call survivors of the bomb, sometimes disdainful, discriminating. But they disdain and discriminate against not only the survivors but against us, too, their children and grandchildren, for fear of the possible effects of the radiation. That's why my grandfather never speaks about that day, she said, and never shows his scars in public.

I was going to tell her that I very much understood the silence of a grandfather survivor, that I very much understood the marks they then wear on their skin for the rest of their lives. But all I did was finish my coffee in that space that was so pleasant, so comfortable. Familiar, almost.

WE'D ALREADY STOOD, were about to head back to the university, when the old man said something to Aiko from his stool, and then the two of them continued speaking in Japanese. But the old man, speaking to Aiko, kept staring at me. His look didn't strike me as judgmental or dismissive, more like a child's stare, sincere yet indiscreet. He wants to know if you're feeling okay, Aiko said. He's a doctor, she said. Or was a doctor. I didn't understand what lay behind his question, but I said yes, I felt fine, thanks. The old man smiled kindly and said something else. He says he doesn't mean to bother you, Aiko told me, but he wants to know if he can take your pulses. Again I didn't understand why, nor did I mind, and I said sure. The old man turned to me, placed three fingers on the inside of my wrist, and left them there, his eyes half-closed. His skin was scaly, his nails long and pointy. I remember I was surprised at his confident yet delicate touch. Why pulses, plural?, I asked Aiko in a whisper, as though not to interrupt the old man's concentration. According to Eastern medicine, she whispered back, we have twenty-nine different pulses. The old man said something brief in Japanese. He says, Aiko told me, he detects a pulse that is like a bowstring, I don't know exactly how to translate the word. Xianmai, the old man said, his fingers still on my wrist (or perhaps not). Xianmai, the pulse is called, Aiko said. Then the old man said something else in Japanese while repeating a strange motion with his other hand. He says, Aiko said, that the rhythm of your pulse is long and tense, like the string of a musical instrument. Ai, the old man said, still stretching the invisible string in the air. Okay, I said, so what does that mean? They spoke for a few seconds. He wants to know if you've recently had any sharp pain in your abdomen, and I said yes, sometimes I did. He wants to know if you've been more tired than usual, and I said yes, in the mornings. He wants to know if you've recently been hit in the belly, and I said no, or I didn't think so (much later I remembered Brussels). The old man said something else.

He says, Aiko said, that this type of pulse can indicate an imbalance in the harmony of your liver or spleen, an imbalance he'd already noticed in the color of your eyes and tone of your skin.

I remained silent, both skeptical and afraid, I suppose. But I don't know whether afraid of the old man himself or of whatever it was that, without stating it explicitly, he was foreseeing. There was no possible way to diagnose all of that by simply taking someone's pulse. Or was there?

The old man suddenly said something brief, categorical, like a final point or a final judgment, and dropped my wrist. But Aiko just thanked him and said goodbye and pushed me toward the exit.

A BUDDHIST MONK WAS WALKING ahead of us. He wore a saffron-colored robe and wooden shoes and protected himself from the elements or the cosmos with an umbrella made of bamboo and white paper. I was sure that seeing him at that moment, right there, in front of us, almost leading us back to the university, was a sign of something. We stopped at an intersection, beside the Buddhist monk, and so I asked Aiko about the last thing the old man had said before letting go of my wrist. She didn't respond. Or maybe she did respond and I couldn't hear her through her mask. I had to ask her to please take it off before I questioned her again about what the old man had said. Nothing important, she said, hidden behind the curtain of her bangs.

THAT AFTERNOON, DURING A TEDIOUS roundtable on the various historical occupations that the Lebanese territory endured (Roman, Ottoman, French, Syrian), and the various and complicated names that its occupiers imposed (the Emirate of Mount Lebanon, the Mutasarrifate of Mount Lebanon, the Syrian State of Greater Lebanon, the United Arab Kingdom of Syria, and finally, officially, the Republic of Lebanon), I kept nodding off and spoke on only one occasion. The Japanese moderator roused me from my siesta to ask what I'd thought of Beirut, the city of my grandfather, the city of my ancestors, and I took the mic and told him I'd never been to Beirut. Though I had been nearby, I said, to Israel. Someone in the audience coughed. Twice, I added, given the total silence in the auditorium. Once for my younger sister's ultra-Orthodox wedding, in Jerusalem. And the other time, when I was twenty, to take part in a sort of Olympics for Jews from all over the world, called the Maccabiah Games, as part of a Jewish Guatemalan basketball team. A circuslike, vaudevillian team of potbellied men and bald men and clumsy old men in bandages moving around with walkers. The thing is, there are almost no Guatemalan Jews to begin with (one hundred families, people say), much less Guatemalan Jews who can dribble a ball with their left hand. Someone in the audience coughed again. We didn't win a single game, I said. But halfway through one game, I nearly came to blows with a Bulgarian player for making fun of us. And I emphatically dropped the mic.

Around me, a few Lebanese brows were still furrowed. I leaned back and crossed my arms and the last thing I thought of—before returning to my siesta—was that the faces in the audience all looked like the expressionless faces in a wax museum.

ANOTHER BREAK MIDAFTERNOON. Another fifteen minutes with Aiko. Possibly the last fifteen minutes alone with her before the last two events, I thought as I saw her walking toward me in her schoolgirl uniform. She was holding two coffees and handed me one. I needed a smoke. I need to find a cigarette, I said, and Aiko immediately turned to a man standing beside her, said something in Japanese, and the man held out a pack and lighter. It was a small pack, apple green in color, with a drawing of two golden bats. Golden Bat, in fact, was what it said in letters of the same gold. I thanked him in English and the man simply bowed his head slightly. You can smoke right out there, in the hallway, Aiko said, and gently took my arm, guiding me like a blind man.

The hallway was loud, warm, hazy, full of smokers. We walked to the end, looking in vain for a bit of privacy, and came to a small rectangular pool made of cement. Peering down into its dark waters, I saw a single koi, long, yellow and white.

Aiko seemed anxious. She stood on tiptoe to get closer to me and asked (her lips almost on my cheek) how many days I was planning to stay in Hiroshima, and I (her cheek almost on my lips) told her I wasn't sure, a few, because after that I wanted to visit Kyoto, see the Kyoto market, spend the night in one of the Buddhist temples. Aiko asked me (her fingers almost on my forearm) if I was interested in seeing an elementary school in Hiroshima, located less than half a kilometer from the site where the bomb was detonated, and I (my fingers almost on her shoulder) said of course. Aiko asked me (her warm breath on my neck) what time my train left the following day, and I (my breath on her warm neck) said quite early. Aiko remained silent a moment. Then her cheeks turned scarlet and her eyes got very sad and she looked as if she was about to start crying right there, amid all the smokers, by the white and yellow koi. And without thinking about it I moved closer to her, maybe to hug her or console her (her breasts almost brushing my chest), maybe just because I wanted to feel her closer (her inner thigh almost tickling mine), and Aiko instinctively backed up, as though defending herself against my indiscretion. I mumbled a few awkward words and distanced myself a bit (gone were the inner thighs and the breasts and the lips and the warmth of our breath). She, her black eyes downcast, shook her head just once, meekly, perhaps saying no with that single movement. Then she went up on tiptoes again and I was sure she wanted to tell me something else, something important, or something ethereal, or something as tiny and fragile as a mockingbird, or something warm to melt that block of ice I'd placed between us, when suddenly the Japanese hierarch came out into the hallway and announced to the smokers that the penultimate event of the afternoon was about to begin.

Everybody went in, except the two of us. The hallway, now, seemed enormous.

Aiko took a timid step toward me. She just stood there, serious, silent. Her eyes looked even blacker. I thought she was offended at my indiscretion, or that she was waiting for me to say something first, maybe a few words about my trip to Hiroshima the next day. But I couldn't say a thing. She reached out a hand and placed it gently on my abdomen and, in a tone of voice I deemed rather urgent or desperate, said to please come with her, that she wanted to show me an ancient tatami made of rice straw and woven with natural fibers from a plant called igusa, which was kept in a private room at the back of the library.

IN THE LATE AFTERNOON, during the final panel, which included all the speakers, my Lebanese disguise began to unravel, to lose its shine.

First, one of the participants, an old novelist from Tripoli, accused me of being an impostor. Or at least that was the word used by the simultaneous interpreter sitting on the stage to my left. Impostor, he said in English. I was unsure whether the old novelist had said it in jest or was serious, and, smiling, I told him that every writer of fiction is an impostor. Then a journalist in jacket and tie announced solemnly—without looking at me—that he couldn't see what sense it made to recount, there, at a conference of Lebanese writers, the story of a Guatemalan farmer and his herd of cows. An older woman, a literature professor, jumped up to defend me, sort of, telling the journalist—also without looking at me and talking about me as if I weren't there—that Halfon did the same thing in his writing, that all his stories seemed to lose the thread and never go anywhere. I didn't say anything, though I could have said this: The photographer Cartier-Bresson, in order to determine the artistic merit of an image, always looked at it upside down. Or I could have said this: The best stories, as Verdi knew, are written in A-flat major. Then a young poet from Beirut came right out and asked if I had ever even tried to visit Lebanon, and when I said that I had not, that it wasn't an easy trip for a Jew, she gave a disgusted look and asked me if I had at least contemplated the possibility of visiting Lebanon. I was about to reply that I had, several times, when the Japanese moderator grabbed the mic in order to save me, and opened the session to questions from the audience. A Japanese woman asked to speak and, attempting to do so with discretion, asked in English why some of the writers present weren't fully Lebanese, asked what criteria the event's organizers had used to select the participants. The Japanese hierarch, from the audience, took the mic and said something about the diversity of Lebanese identity, its not being limited to a single country or language. Sitting to my right, a famous writer, who was Brazilian, though born in Beirut, leaned over to me and whispered that all Lebanese people invent their own personal Lebanon, because Lebanon as a country doesn't actually exist, and

155

it struck me that the same could be said about Guatemala. Some of the writers on the panel were already making pronouncements in Arabic, clearly disagreeing with the hierarch, and although the simultaneous interpreter went on interpreting for me in whispers, I decided it was best not to pay attention anymore and simply looked out the only window in the auditorium: an enormous picture window with panoramic views of the city (just in front of the glass, I realized, stood the black-and-white balloon, still in his chauffeur's uniform and with his hands behind his back but now wearing a vaguely delighted or vengeful expression, perhaps just waiting for it all to end to take me somewhere far from there). The famous Brazilian writer, beside me, was lightly patting my forearm in apparent compassion and solidarity. The others continued arguing in Arabic, ever louder, some even pointing at me, and I continued staring out the window at the city. But slowly, as the Arabic arguments ratcheted up and the public incinerated me with their eyes (or that's the way it appeared to me), I began to feel a pressing need not only to explain myself but to defend myself from so much suspicion and indictment. The Beirut poet was gesticulating and shouting something in Arabic—possibly one of her poems—when I began to speak without even asking permission or requesting the microphone.

I spoke about my grandfather. I spoke about my grandfather's house. I spoke about my grandfather's siblings. I spoke about my grandfather's business in Paris. I spoke about my grandfather's kidnapping. I spoke about one of my grandfather's kidnappers. I spoke about my grandfather's death. I spoke about my grandfather saying things that I was making up on the spot. I was making everything up on the spot. But it didn't matter. It no longer mattered to me what I said about my grandfather, whether what I said about my grandfather was truthful or even relevant, only that I not stop talking about him, and thereby not allow my compatriots and colleagues to again take the floor and keep accusing me of being an impostor and a traitor and whatever else. Several times they tried to interrupt me or stop me, but I just kept speaking loudly about my grandfather. And I said even more about my grandfather. And I was still speaking about my grandfather when I realized that the enormous window had gone dark, and that on the other side the lights of Tokyo were illuminating the night, and that in its reflection the golden sequins on my costume were once again beginning to shine.

Bellevue Literary Press is devoted to publishing
literary fiction and nonfiction at the intersection of
the arts and sciences because we believe that science
and the humanities are natural companions for
understanding the human experience.
We feature exceptional literature that explores
the nature of consciousness, embodiment, and
the underpinnings of the social contract. With
each book we publish, our goal is to foster a rich,
interdisciplinary dialogue that will forge new
tools for thinking and engaging with the world.

To support our press and its mission, and for
our full catalogue of published titles, please visit
us at blpress.org.

BELLEVUE LITERARY PRESS
New York